THE TOFF IN TO

John Creasey

The Toff in Town

WALKER AND COMPANY
New York

B -2

First published in the United States of America 1977 by the Walker Publishing Company, Inc.

ISBN: 0-8027-5380-9

Library of Congress Catalog Card Number: 77-80630

Printed in the United States of America

10 9 8 7 6 5 4 3 2 1

CHAPTER ONE

FEAR

WHEN the telephone bell rang, Allen sat hunched up in an easy chair, looking out of the window. His wife was entering the room, and saw him stiffen and glance round. She said: 'I'll go.' She caught a glimpse of the fear in her husband's eyes before he turned away again and looked over the roof-tops and the chimneys. The telephone bell kept ringing.

'Well, go on, if you're going,' Allen said gruffly.

His wife went into the tiny hall and took up the receiver but did not speak immediately, her heart was beating so fast. Fear was contagious, and Bob was so terribly afraid. At last she spoke in a low-pitched voice.

'Barbara Allen speaking.'

'Good-morning, Mrs. Allen,' a man said. 'May I speak to your husband?'

'Yes. Just a moment.'

The voice was familiar. Mellow, pleasant, friendly, yet whenever Bob received a message from this man, whom she did not know, his fear reached a pitch which drove him almost to frenzy. But she wasn't going to quarrel with Bob again, he wasn't well—neither physically nor mentally well.

'It's for you,' called Barbara.

He came into the hall, staring hard at her, and drew back, as if he were going to refuse to take the call. Then he moved forward, limping noticeably, and took the receiver from her.

'Allen speaking,' he said gruffly.

He stood still, looking blankly at a black-and-white drawing of a thatched cottage on the wall. Barbara saw the naked fear in his eyes—and noticed the little pulse beating in his neck.

'Yes,' he said; the word came out sharply.

A pause, and then: 'But surely Saturday——'

He broke off. Barbara could just hear the other man's voice coming from the receiver, but she could not distinguish the words. Bob's left hand was clenching and unclenching. It

7

seemed a long time before he replaced the receiver, after a reluctant: 'All right.'

He turned back to the sitting-room.

'Bob,' said Barbara.

'Oh, don't pester me!' he snapped.

She tried to stifle the little catch in her breath, almost a sob, but didn't succeed, and Allen paused in the doorway and looked round. His eyes were haunted. His face was so thin and long, there were dark patches beneath his eyes; his mouth, wide and generous and droll at ordinary times, was set tightly. He paused as if to speak to her, but changed his mind. He didn't close the door.

Barbara composed herself and went into the small kitchen.

She'd known happiness reach a point of ecstasy here; and despair; and contentment. She had been standing by the sink when the telegram had arrived announcing that her husband was missing—from a flight in Burma. She had been taking some rock cakes out of the oven when another telegram had come—only three months ago, many years after he had been 'lost' and 'presumed dead'. It had read:

'*Your husband alive and well.*'

Ecstasy . . .

And now she despaired again.

'Alive and well' had been an exaggeration, even then; he had been weak after living for years with natives in an unexplored, inaccessible part of Burma. When she had reached Burma by air and seen him, she had hardly recognised him, partly because he was in the middle of a bout of malaria. But not until they had been half-way home, in the ship, had these fits of fear taken hold of him. She put them down to some evil memory held deep in the dark recesses of his mind; but they had become worse, far worse.

Each day the same man had telephoned.

This was the first time that she hadn't asked afterwards: 'Bob, tell me what it's about, what's worrying you,' and thus precipitated a scene. She was determined to wait until he was ready to confide in her; they couldn't go on like this.

She lit the grill; air got into the gas and hissed, and she turned the tap off. In the little silence which followed she heard a footstep, and looked into the hall. Bob's hand was outstretched, reaching for his hat. When he saw her, he snatched his hat off the peg.

8

'Bob!' she exclaimed.

'I'm going out,' he said harshly. 'Won't be long.'

Her good intentions failed her, and she hurried out into the hall.

'Bob, you must tell me——'

'We're not going into that again,' he growled.

She hated the way he looked at her, and yet she knew he saw something else, not her face, but the thing which frightened him.

She felt suddenly cool, calm and decided.

'Yes, we are going into that again,' she insisted. 'If you leave without telling me what that man said, what's worrying you so much, I'm going to take things into my own hands.'

He fiddled with the brim of his hat.

'Well, what are you going to do about it?' he demanded. She knew that he could hardly speak civilly; he began to tremble, as if another bout of malaria were coming on, but it was only the tension.

'I'm going to the police,' she declared. 'I'm going to tell them that you——'

He flung his hat aside and crossed the hall, and she hardly noticed his limp. He clutched her wrists; his fingers were long and powerful and he hurt her. His eyes blazed, as they always did when he flew into a temper. He pulled her to him, and their faces were very close together.

'Don't say that again,' he rasped. 'Don't you dare go to the police. Understand me?'

She didn't try to get away, but spoke quietly, keeping unnaturally calm.

'If you leave without telling me what's worrying you, I shall go to the police and tell them that since you've been back in England you've been—terrified. I shall tell them about the man on the telephone, and I shall say that I'm afraid you'll do something desperate if you don't get help.'

His grip was so tight that the pain almost made her cry out, but she clenched her teeth and returned his furious gaze. The little vein in his neck beat furiously, his lips were compressed into a thin line, his nostrils distended.

'You—wouldn't—dare!'

'I shall,' she insisted.

'You mustn't go to the police,' he said in a low-pitched voice, and although she hardly understood why, she had a

9

feeling that something had changed within him, too. 'I shall be all right, I shan't make a fool of myself. It—it won't last for ever.'

'It's lasted too long,' she said.

Suddenly he let her go and pushed her away.

'Then clear out!' he shouted. 'Clear out! You're tired of me, you're tired of a sick husband, of a physical wreck. You haven't any patience left, you hate the sight of me. Clear out, I tell you! You've still got youth and beauty on your side, plenty of men——'

'Bob!'

'Plenty of men would find you worth bedding,' he went on almost hysterically. 'Men who stayed at home, men who weren't hurt, the men who gave you a good time while I——'

She slapped him across the face.

He backed away and his right hand rose slowly to his cheek, fingering the spot where she had hit him. There was something akin to wonder in his eyes; at least she had driven that devouring fear away, if only for a few minutes.

Suddenly he turned away.

'Oh, God!' he groaned. 'I'm sorry. But it's no use. I'm no good to you. I never will be. But it's my trouble, not yours. You shouldn't try to share it.' He limped across to his hat, stooped down and picked it up. 'The advice was sound. You'd better leave me, Bar.'

'I shan't leave you,' said Barbara quietly. 'I've told you what I shall do.'

He shook his head, turning to face her.

'You mustn't go to the police,' he said. 'That tells you plenty, doesn't it? I am afraid of the police as well as a lot of other things. But I'm not going to tell you why, nothing will drag it out of me. I'm not going to involve you.'

'But, Bob, surely—surely you know that if you're in trouble, I can't keep *out*.'

'You needn't jump in with both feet.' Allen's voice was harsh and dry. 'Stop this idea of the police, Bar. It won't help. Might do a lot more harm. I've a chance of getting through. Saturday should tell.'

'Saturday?' She felt a flare of hope. '*This* Saturday?'

'Yes. So *he* said. Believe it or not, I don't know him, but he knows a lot about me. Knows I once did a crazy thing.' He paused. 'Forget it until Saturday. I'll try to behave like a

10

rational human being until then.'

It was tempting to press questions because he was in a mood when he might talk freely. On the other hand, they might send him back into his shell again, and this was the first time he had talked about it at all. She forced herself to accept his mood.

'All right, darling,' she said. 'I will.'

The 'darling' brought a hoarse cry to his lips. He gripped her hands again and this time pulled her close; they strained against each other. His hands played with her hair, with her shoulders, his fingers pressing deep into her flesh. When at last he let her go, a ghost of the old smile played at the corner of his lips and there was a brighter light in his eyes.

'Believe it or not,' he said, 'I love you.'

'Talking of my foul innuendo, as one might say, ever see anything of Snub these days?' asked Allen.

They were in the sitting-room. The sun had broken through the clouds, brightening the red of nearby chimneys and the blue tiles of the block of flats opposite. In the distance some trees were touched with gold. The view from the flat had never looked better; and not since his return, had Barbara felt so light-hearted. He had been almost himself for nearly an hour.

'Snub?' echoed Barbara.

'Snub Higginbottom,' said Allen, grinning. 'Don't say you've forgotten——'

'Oh, *Snub*!' Her eyes lit up. 'The last time he came up, was just after you'd been reported missing. What on earth made you think of him?'

'I caught sight of him in Regent Street the other day,' said Allen. 'He was with one of those *Tailor-and-Cutter* types—I thought they'd died with the war. Didn't see me. And I saw something about him in one of those old newspapers I've been reading—to try to bring myself up to date. Snub gave evidence in a nasty murder case, apparently he had quite a time. Useful chap, in a tight corner.' He did not appear to be thinking of his own tight corner. 'Well, what shall we do this afternoon?'

'Anything you like!'

Allen gave her a meaning grin.

'That's dangerous, ducky, in my present sentimental mood! But let's go out. Let's——'

The telephone bell rang again.

His lips clamped together and he glanced towards the hall.

11

The first 'ting' had brought everything back vividly, and Barbara had come to hate the telephone. Neither of them got up, and the bell kept ringing. Then they started to move together, and Barbara reached her feet first. But Allen said:

'No, I'll go.'

He limped into the hall.

He had broken his leg when he had crashed on the flight which had nearly ended his life, and the natives who had rescued him had set the bone badly. There was some talk of having it broken and re-set, but he hadn't shown much interest in that or in anything else, except—fear and the mellow-voiced man.

'Allen speaking,' he said harshly. There was an agonising pause; she did not move, felt numbed and stiff. Then he went on in a completely different voice in which there was a throb of excitement. 'You want me to *what?*'

Barbara jumped up and rushed into the hall. He looked round at her, obviously excited, and mouthed the word: 'Quiet.' She waited, close by his side, and he kept saying: 'Yes, if you like,' over and over again. Then at last he said decidedly: 'No, not to-morrow, I'm engaged all day to-morrow. I *could* manage this afternoon, if that's any good . . . Right-ho! Where is it? . . . Aeolian Hall, New Bond Street, yes, I've got that, and I ask for . . . Mr Hedley . . . Right, thanks, good-bye!'

He rang off, and stared at Barbara with his eyes glistening.

'Well, what do you make of *that*,' he demanded.

'Bob, what is it?'

'Fame in a night!' cried Allen. 'A three minutes' wonder! That was the B.B.C.! A man named Hedley thinks I can fill up a gap in the *In Town To-night* show. Saturday,' he added. 'He wants to see me beforehand. I wouldn't go to-morrow because you and I are having a day in the country.'

'Bob, it's glorious!'

'Oh, I don't know about that,' he said, more calmly. 'I shall be as nervous as Old Harry. Still——' A shadow entered his eyes as he went on: 'Saturday will be quite a day, won't it?'

CHAPTER TWO

FRIGHT

THE little chiming clock in the sitting-room struck four. Barbara heard it as she sat in the bedroom, putting on lipstick. 'I must hurry,' she thought, but she didn't hurry; she finished with the lipstick and looked at her face, carefree for the first time for weeks. She looked better, too; the little furrow between her eyes, which had become almost permanent, had gone. And this bright green suited her; it was a smart suit, and the wide-brimmed hat had gone on just right. She ought to have a set, but her hair wasn't *too* bad. She tucked in a few light brown strands, and then suddenly laughed aloud.

Everything would be all right!

Anxiety hadn't quite gone; Bob had been too emphatic about the police, as if some crime were heavy on his conscience, but he had been transformed, almost normal, since the call from the B.B.C. Bob to broadcast! Would she be able to go with him? Or would it be better to hear him on their own radio? She glanced at it, where it stood on the bedside table, then stepped across the room and picked up the *Radio Times*. She turned over the pages to Saturday and read:

6.15 p.m. *In Town To-night.*
400 Edition.
Once again we stop the mighty roar of London's traffic and bring to you some of the interesting people who are in town to-night.

She put the paper down, and saw a small slip of paper on the floor. It was yellow with age, and when she picked it up, she saw some shorthand notes on it. She couldn't make out the meaning, but it was obviously too old to matter. She screwed it up and tossed it into the waste-paper basket, then went across and glanced at herself in the mirror again, satisfied that she looked her best.

It had been impossible to judge how long Bob would be, so they had arranged to meet outside the Aeolian Hall at half-past four. She had only twenty minutes to get there from St. John's Wood; she shouldn't have had a bath. She picked up her hand-bag and gloves, and stepped into the hall.

The front door bell rang.

'Oh, bother!' she exclaimed.

Even if the caller only delayed her for a few minutes, she could now no longer hope to be in New Bond Street at half-past four. She hurried to the door and opened it briskly. Then looked in surprise at two men—one little more than a boy. They were dressed in blue overalls, and one of them carried a rope-bag.

'Good-afternoon,' said Barbara.

'Afternoon, Miss. Come about the gas.'

'Gas?' echoed Barbara. 'I haven't sent——'

Then a great fear welled up in her, for the bigger of the two lunged forward. He had something in his hands—a large sponge. While that stab of fear was making her heart swell, and pain shot across her breast, he thrust the sponge into her face. She caught a whiff of a penetrating smell which took her breath away. Her hands were gripped from behind, and she felt herself dragged into the hall. She couldn't see; something was burning her face, a cloud was filling her mind, it was as if she were breathing in smoke, dense black smoke. Then she couldn't breathe at all. She retched. The pressure on her arms increased, the burning sensation was unbearable, but—it didn't last long. That great black cloud enshrouded her, all other pain was lost in the agony of choking, she seemed to be rising from the floor.

She felt sick.

She *was* sick . . .

She lay back exhausted. There was something hard beneath her head. She couldn't see properly because of a mist in front of her eyes. She felt the awful nausea in her stomach, and her lips and nose were sore—terribly sore; burning.

The mist receded.

She was in the hall, lying on the floor. She could see Bob's mackintosh and overcoat hanging on the hall-stand, and the black and white country scene on the wall.

She remembered.

Another spasm of fear clutched at her, as if a hand were gripping at her inside and twisting, but she struggled to get up. One shoe was off, lying near the hall-stand. Her gloves were by her side, her hand-bag was lying open, and all the contents

14

were strewn about the floor.

She stood up.

She caught sight of herself, as she swayed forward, in the hall-stand mirror. Her lipstick was smeared and she was very red about the nose and mouth—but that wasn't *all* lipstick; something had burned her. She saw something else. The buttons of her white blouse were undone. She shivered involuntarily, *she* hadn't done that. What had happened? What *had* happened to her? Those two men——

She made herself go into the sitting-room, but was exhausted when she reached the nearest chair, and sank into it. The clock began to strike, She missed counting the first. Four—not four, she had heard four. It was—nearly six o'clock, the hands wouldn't keep steady. It *was* six o'clock.

She was an hour and a half late. Bob—why hadn't he returned? Was he still waiting for her? She remembered everything clearly now, but even anxiety about Bob faded into the background. Recollection of the way that man had darted forward and thrust the sponge over her face made her shudder again.

Bob would come back soon, he'd realise that something had gone wrong.

After a while she got up. The burning on her face was very painful, she must bathe it. She went into the bath-room and sprinkled some boracic powder into the hand-basin and bathed her lips and nose, but it didn't help much. They were puffy and swollen and there was a foul taste in her mouth. She had been chloroformed, she realised. Chloroformed, and——

She looked down at her blouse.

Only now did she realise that everything in the first-aid cabinet had been moved. Several things, including Bob's shaving tackle were on the floor. She couldn't understand it—but understanding dawned when she returned to the sitting-room, feeling no better, but at least able to see and to take notice. The contents of a writing-table were strewn on the top, the drawer of a card-table was lying on the floor, and the contents were scattered all over the carpet. She made herself go into the bedroom and the tiny dining-room, and found everything in chaos. The fact that it would take hours to straighten every-thing hardly occurred to her. She ought to tell the police.

Then she remembered what Bob had said about them.

Why hadn't he come back?

15

She rinsed her mouth out with cold water, using a mouthwash tablet. Thieves, police, Bob. She went into the hall and looked at the telephone—and it rang!

The sound startled her so much that she jumped and backed away, knocking her head against the wall. The bell went on ringing. She trembled as she stepped towards it, and the receiver quivered in her hand. Her voice was no more than a husky whisper.

'Can't hear you.' The voice at the other end of the line was sharp, unfamiliar, impatient.

'Mrs.—Allen—speaking.'

'Okay,' the man said. 'Your husband's been delayed. Might not be home until late.'

'Is that the B.B.C.?' she asked, but there was no answer, and she heard the receiver go down at the other end. She held hers in her hand for some seconds, then slowly put it back. Bob delayed, might not be home until late. But—that voice, it hadn't been a B.B.C. voice! In a sudden frenzy she picked up the directory. Her fingers trembled, she kept fumbling for the 'B's', found them at last and after a frantic search, found: 'British Broadcasting Corporation.' She didn't want Broadcasting House—Aeolian Hall, there it was.

She dialled.

'B.B.C.,' said a girl crisply.

'May I—may I speak to Mr. Hedley?'

'I'm sorry, I can't hear you very well. Mr. Who?'

'Mr. *Hedley*!' She shouted this time, her voice suddenly strong, and the operator said: 'I'll see if he's in his office.' She held on for a long time, and began to think that she had been forgotten, when the girl spoke again. 'I'm sorry, he's left the building.'

'Are you—sure?'

'Yes, I'm afraid so.' Bless that girl, she wasn't curt, she was helpful.

Barbara said: 'I'm sorry to be a nuisance, but my husband had an appointment with Mr. Hedley this afternoon and—and I want to know whether he's left.'

'What name is it, please?'

'Allen—Robert Allen.'

'I *might* be able to find out,' said the girl. 'Hold on, please.'

There was another long wait. Barbara hooked a chair with her foot, drew it close to the table and sat down. She felt so

16

weak. It was half-past six now.

'Hallo,' said the girl.

'*Yes!*'

'Mr. Allen left just after four o'clock,' the operator reported. 'I've spoken to someone who was in the office at the time. I'm sorry.'

'That's—all right,' said Barbara. 'Thank you very much.'

She replaced the receiver and stared blankly in front of her. If Bob hadn't been detained at the B.B.C., who had telephoned to say that he would be late? Where was he? The mystery which created his fear and her unhappiness closed down upon her.

Bob hadn't returned at nine o'clock.

Barbara had not left the flat, had spoken to no one. Wearily at first, she had tidied up; the rooms were more or less in order now. She couldn't think of anything that was missing. The few pounds, the ready money she always kept tucked away in a drawer, had been on the floor; if the thieves had wanted to take money, why hadn't they taken that? Her few oddments of jewellery were still on the dressing-table. All her clothes and Bob's were there, and yet the man had searched every nook and cranny, even the larder.

The wa..e-paper basket overflowed with oddments of paper, old powder-puffs, an accumulation of rubbish. She emptied the basket into the fireplace, and put a match to them, then watched them flare up.

She felt better, and rather hungry. She made herself some tea and ate some biscuits—the tin lid had been left off by the intruders. The tea was hot and stung her lips and mouth, so she cooled it with more milk. Her face was badly swollen but not so sore. She had done her hair and wiped off her lipstick; she looked a sight, but that didn't matter.

What had the man meant by 'late'?

Was it 'late' now?

If only Bob hadn't been so insistent about not going to the police, she would have telephoned them, but she could not doubt that the burglary was connected with the mystery, and she couldn't let him down. But if he didn't return soon, she'd *have* to telephone Scotland Yard. How long dare she leave it? Until ten o'clock?

Or eleven?

At half-past ten she went into the bedroom, aimlessly, perhaps partly to keep away from the telephone. Ringing up the police and reporting that Bob was missing seemed the only thing to do, but—was he really missing yet? How she hated that word! *'Missing—feared dead.'* She went to the other side of the bed, Bob's side, and saw the old newspapers on the chair, a pile of them. He had managed to get some back numbers of Sunday papers; he had been hungry for news of what had happened while he had been away.

She remembered their talk after lunch about Snub Higginbottom, a useful man in a tight corner. In a frenzy, she picked up the newspapers and spread them out over the bed. If she couldn't consult the police, she *must* talk to someone. She went through paper after paper, looking for headlines about a murder trial. It took a long time, and she was in her own light, her shadow darkened the pages. She might have missed——

There it was!

In evidence, Mr. James Higginbottom said . . .

She skimmed what he had said as she searched for his address; she did not find it, but there was an address further down the page.

The Hon. Richard Rollison, of Gresham Terrace, W.1., gave evidence of finding the body. Mr. Rollison . . .

She didn't trouble to read on from there, but went into the hall and looked for 'Higginbottom' in the directory. There were several, but she couldn't be sure which was James or 'Snub'. She looked for Rollison. The entry was there all right, *'Rollison, R. The Hon., 55g, Gresham Terrace, Mayfair . . .*

CHAPTER THREE

HELPING HAND

It was some time before a man with a deep voice announced: 'Rollison here.'

'I—I'm sorry to worry you,' said Barbara. 'Can you please tell me where to find Mr. Higginbottom? Mr. James Higginbottom? I think—you once——'

'I know Mr. Higginbottom,' said the man with the deep voice, 'and I can give you his address, but you won't find him in to-night, I'm afraid.'

'Oh no,' said Barbara.

All her dismay and despair sounded in that single exclamation.

'Perhaps I can help you,' the man suggested.

'I—I don't think so,' said Barbara. 'I just wanted——' She couldn't go on.

'I might be able to get in touch with Mr. Higginbottom, if it's really urgent,' said Rollison.

He sounded friendly and anxious to help, and she couldn't stop herself from bursting out:

'Oh, it is!'

'Then give me your name and telephone number,' said Rollison. 'You would like to see him to-night, I imagine?'

'Oh, yes, please.' She gave him the details. 'It doesn't matter how late it is, I shan't be able to rest until I've seen him.'

'If I were you, I'd try,' advised Rollison.

She rang off, and smiling wanly at the recollection of his advice, went into the bedroom, kicked off her shoes, and lay down. The man had sounded so calm and reassuring that she began to wonder if she were making too much fuss. Bob might return soon. It wasn't yet late; not really late.

Richard Rollison stood up from his desk in his large study-cum-sitting-room, and, without looking at the papers which he had been reading, went into the hall.

This was quite roomy and furnished sparsely, although a connoisseur would have appreciated the old oak settle with a swing seat, and the near-black wardrobe, the small but exquisite water-colours on the walls. A thick-pile brown carpet covered the floor. A short passage led off the hall to his man's room, the kitchen and the bath-room. The main rooms all led from the hall.

He called out: 'Asleep yet, Jolly?' and his man answered in a sleepy voice: 'No, sir, not at all.' Rollison smothered a grin and opened the door.

By day, Jolly always dressed in black. By night, his colour scheme was much more gay, and he wore bright yellow pyjamas which were somewhat unexpected in a room which was obviously a man's. It was rather crowded, with good but not antique furniture, and one wall was lined with books.

The light from a bedside lamp reflected from the yellow

19

garments and gave his lined face, with its dewlaps, a look of yellow jaundice. He had been reading, in bed, and struggled to sit up while retaining hold on his book.

'Let me help you,' said Rollison gravely.

'I can manage quite well, sir, thank you,' said Jolly. 'I must have been nearly asleep,' he remarked. 'I'm sorry sir.'

'I wish I were nearly asleep,' said Rollison smiling into Jolly's brown, soulful-looking eyes. 'But I'm going out.'

'Can I get you anything?' asked Jolly.

'I hope I'm not going to need anything,' said Rollison. 'Jolly, between these four walls——'

'Yes, sir?' A hopeful, inquiring note sprang into Jolly's voice.

'Snub isn't in love or anything like that, is he?' asked Rollison.

'Mr. Higginbottom, sir? I have not been informed of any such phenomenon.' Jolly was now quite wide awake. 'He does from time to time form attachments, but I believe they are always short-lived.'

'But how deep while they last? Has he ever mentioned a Mrs. Allen?'

Jolly pondered, and shook his head. 'I don't recall the name, sir.'

'Or Barbara Allen? Possibly shortened to Bar or Babs?'

'Definitely not, sir,' said Jolly. 'I hope that Mr. Higginbottom has not been getting himself into difficulties.'

'So do I,' said Rollison. 'But a tearful young lady wants to see him urgently, and doesn't mind how late it is when he calls. She's undoubtedly in trouble. Snub's in Blackpool, disporting himself with the Lancashire lasses, and so——'

'You are going to see Mrs. Allen,' concluded Jolly.

'Admirable deduction,' said Rollison. 'And I'm going at once because I don't want to be too late! Her address is Byngham—with a "y"—Court Mansions, St. John's Wood, and her telephone number is St. John's 81312. So if I'm not back by the morning, you'll know where to find me.'

'Very good, sir,' said Jolly primly.

'Good-night,' said Rollison.

After Rollison had gone, Jolly shook his head and smiled —a rather solemn smile, as one might give when brooding over the follies of youth or the idiosyncracies of men in love. He knew that Rollison had lately been lured into a series of social functions which he seldom enjoyed, and this was his first early night for a week. Moreover, Rollison—sometimes called the Toff—did not make up in the morning for sleep he lost at night. He was busy with a variety of jobs, many self-imposed, and missed the services of Snub Higginbottom, his secretary.

The unexpected visit had driven sleep away. Jolly got up, put on a dark blue dressing-gown, made himself a cup of tea, and took it into the study. He enjoyed an hour there when Rollison was not in. To-night, he found himself contemplating the trophy wall.

At one time he had disapproved of it, for the trophies were not of ordinary hunts, but of man-hunts. And in most of them Jolly had played a part, not always willing, but often important. There were, for instance, the two umbrella-handles. With one, Jolly had hooked the feet from under a man who might easily have mortally wounded his employer; with the other, Jolly had knocked a man out simply by striking him over the head. Curiously enough, these incidents were the only ones for which Jolly had been formally thanked by a magistrate or a judge for contributing to the success of the law over lawlessness, which was why Rollison had selected them as Jolly's trophies.

There was the top hat, right at the top, with a hole drilled through the crown. There were chicken feathers. There were knives, automatics, curious and ingenious weapons, some of which hardly looked lethal. There were glass cases in which were tiny quantities of deadly poisons. There was a cosh, one of the earliest trophies; it was after Rollison had won the cosh, that Jolly had first heard him called 'The Toff'. And there was a visiting-card—one of Rollison's, with spots of dried blood on one side and, on the other, a simple drawing of a top-hat, a monocle and a swagger cane. The Toff seldom used such a card these days——

Jolly sipped his tea, and remembered.

At five minutes past twelve, the front door bell at No. 31, Byngham Court Mansions rang. Barbara, still on the bed, sat up abruptly, and her heart began to thump. It wasn't Bob, he had a key. The last time the front door bell had rung, she had opened it to admit the two 'workmen'. Getting up, she glanced in the mirror, but there was nothing she could do about her appearance, her lips and nose were even puffier now. She hurried out and opened the front door.

The hall light shone on a tall, dark-haired man. She saw in

the first glimpse that he was good-looking, and she liked the way his lips curved. He wore a light-coloured raincoat but no hat. He wasn't Snub Higginbottom. Snub had earned his name through the shape of his nose, and this man's nose was aquiline. Then she saw his eyes; grey, clear, with a curious brilliance.

'Mrs. Allen?' It was the voice she had heard over the telephone.

'You—you've come yourself!' She stood aside, and was vividly aware of his searching glance. What should she tell him now that he was here? She hadn't dreamed he would come himself, and it would have been difficult enough to tell Higginbottom, who had known Bob for years.

The stranger closed the door gently.

'You've had a rough time,' he remarked. 'Nasty stuff, chloroform.'

'Chloro——' she began, and choked on the word.

'When carelessly applied, it has a colourful effect. I can smell it, too,' said Rollison. He gave her another penetrating stare, yet his eyes had softened. 'Are you alone here?'

'Yes. My husband—hasn't come back. That's why——'

And suddenly it was easy to talk.

When she had finished the story, Rollison was sitting in Bob's easy chair and Barbara in a fireside shair, hugging her knees. She had started off by intending to tell him a little—about the attack on her and Bob's long absence, but he prompted her so shrewdly that she kept nothing back. One of his comments had been: 'I'm not a policeman, you know,' and that had done more than anything else to make her talk without reticence.

Now that all was told, she still felt desperately anxious, but relieved. He offered her cigarettes, then laughed at himself because obviously she couldn't smoke with any enjoyment. His naturalness won her completely.

'But you smoke, please,' she said.

'Thanks.' Rollison lit a cigarette. 'Did anyone else know where your husband was going?'

'No, not a soul. There was hardly time to tell anyone. In any case, the people in the next flat are away, and we don't know them downstairs, they're comparatively new.'

'How new?' asked Rollison quickly.

'Well—six or seven months.'

'They came before your husband returned?'

'Oh yes, some time before.'

Rollison lost interest in the 'new' people downstairs.

'The men who telephoned to say your husband would be late must know where he is,' reasoned Rollison. 'Cases of kidnapping in broad daylight are rare, it's much more likely that someone persuaded him to go with them, and although he may not have gone willingly, he probably went of his own volition. What time did the gas-men come?'

'At ten past four exactly.'

'A gas-man and his mate are among the least noticed people in London,' remarked Rollison. 'I suppose you haven't noticed anyone loitering about the street outside in the last few days?'

'No, no one,' said Barbara, after a moment's reflection.

'Other people may have noticed them. Have you any idea what they wanted?'

'No,' answered Barbara.

'Sure? Not even a notion?'

'Yes, I'm quite sure.' The importance of the question struck home to Barbara now. 'Bob told me nothing at all until this morning, when—well, I've told *you*——' She broke off, leaning back and half-closing her eyes. 'And all I know is, he's afraid of the police and—and *hopes* that he'll have nothing to worry about after Saturday.' Rollison nodded understanding, and she went on: 'I can't imagine why he should be so frightened of the police. I can't imagine Bob committing a crime, or even thinking of it.'

'Let's not forget that he had several very rough years, and when a man comes out of the hell that's Burma jungle, he isn't going to be quite himself for some time,' said Rollison. 'And like a lot of people he may be more nervous of the police than necessary. They're not so bad, you know. Human beings and all that kind of thing. No malice or vindictiveness. I have known people nearly off their heads with worry, when ten minutes with a detective-sergeant would have set their minds at rest.'

'You're like a breath of fresh air!' exclaimed Barbara.

'You want something to blow the cobwebs away,' said Rollison.

As he finished speaking, there was a faint sound somewhere in the flat. Barbara hardly noticed it as she studied him. He had brought calm and commonsense to bear on her problem, and she felt soothed and reassured.

When the noise was repeated, she noticed it.

Rollison's smile remained, but a little vertical furrow appeared between his eyes. Barbara opened her lips to speak, but he raised his hand for silence.

'What——' she began huskily.

'Hush,' murmured Rollison. He put his hands on the arm of his chair and stood up, a swift movement. He looked towards the closed door, and when the sound came again.

'What room is next door?' asked Rollison softly.

'The—the kitchen.'

'And a door to the fire-escape is there?'

'Yes.' She caught her breath.

'Is the kitchen door open or closed?' As he asked that, he approached her. 'Don't get worked up. This may be a false alarm—or it may be just the thing to put us right. Is the kitchen door——'

'It's closed.'

'Good, said Rollison. 'I'm going to put the light out. Just stay where you are, I'll be back in a moment.'

He crossed the room and put his hand to the switch; there was a faint click, and the light went out. Barbara stood in the darkness, staring towards the door. She heard it open and thought there was a faint creak as Rollison went out. A second creak was much louder; the kitchen door squeaked, he was opening that. A moment later a window rattled—very loudly.

It kept rattling, as if a high wind were buffeting it, but the window of the sitting-room didn't move, so it couldn't be the wind.

CHAPTER FOUR

INTRUDER

INSIDE the flat all was quiet. Rollison stood by the kitchen door, seeing the outline of the window and the starlit sky beyond— and the head and shoulders of a man outside.

He waited only long enough to convince himself that a man was standing on the fire-escape, then closed the door. The key was on the outside; he turned it, and went back to the sitting-room. He could just make out Barbara Allen, standing in front of her chair.

'Can you see me?' he called softly.

'Ju—just,' she answered unsteadily.

'A man's trying to get in,' said Rollison in a matter-of-fact voice. 'Will you do exactly what I tell you?'

'Yes.'

'Then go to your bedroom, undress and get into bed,' said Rollison. 'He's probably come to question you, as the flat's already been searched. We might find out what he's after. You've several minutes to get ready, I've locked the kitchen door. All clear?'

'Yes,' whispered Barbara. She was shivering.

'We might find out what's behind it all,' Rollison said. 'He won't dream that I'm listening. Which is your bedroom?'

'Opposite this room.' She was calmer now; he'd given her both confidence and hope.

'Good—come on,' said Rollison.

He drew to one side as she came towards him, her figure a clear silhouette against the window. She made no fuss, passed him and went through a doorway—he couldn't see her then. The bedroom door closed. The rattling at the window stopped and after a pause he heard a thud; the man was now in the kitchen.

There was no sound at all from the bedroom.

Rollison backed towards the telephone, groped cautiously, touched the table, pressed close to the wall and squeezed into a recess.

Scratching sounds at the door told him that the intruder was working on the lock. Soon, the kitchen door squeaked open loudly.

The light from a torch flashed on, striking the wall opposite, and was reflected from the glass of one of the small pictures. The intruder lowered it and moved it round slowly. It shone on the telephone, and Rollison, pressing tightly against the wall, prepared to act if he were seen.

The beam of light moved away, missing him, and made a complete circuit of the hall until finally it came to rest on the bedroom door-handle. The circle of light on the door grew larger, and in the reflection Rollison could just make out the man's figure. The light grew whiter as the torch drew closer to the wall. Suddenly part of it was hidden by the man's figure. A short, squat fellow, he moved with great stealth. The shadow of his hands appeared on the door as he changed the torch

25

from his left hand to his right, he wore dark gloves.

The light shone brightly on the handle now.

Fingers closed round it, and turned. The door opened slowly, and the light grew dim as the beam shone into the room and was dispersed. The man went in, clearly visible against the torch beam.

Would he close the door?

He didn't, but disappeared from view; now Rollison could see only a faint glow of light. He stepped forward gently, peering through the crack between the door and the wall. The torch shone on Barbara's head and the pillow. She lay on her side, facing the wall—and the man would have to go to the other side of the bed in order to examine her face closely.

Rollison stopped in the doorway as a gloved hand went over Barbara's mouth, to stifle any cry.

'Wake up!' the burglar said harshly.

Barbara turned her head.

Rollison withdrew, and watched through the crack, able to hear every sound.

'*Wake up!*' the man repeated, shaking her.

Barbara 'woke up'; Rollison heard a stifled gasp, and saw her start. Next moment a brighter light shone; the intruder had switched on the bedside lamp.

'What—what——' Barbara gasped.

'Don't make a sound,' the man ordered. 'Sit up.'

Barbara struggled to a sitting position, staring at him with puzzled, frightened eyes; she looked as if she had just been awakened out of a deep sleep. Her mouth was rounded in an 'O' of fright, she held her hands in front of her breasts. Her hair was tousled, she wore a flimsy silk nightdress or pyjamas.

'What——' she began again.

'Shut up!' The intruder's voice was grating and unpleasant; he made a powerful, menacing figure. 'Just answer my questions.' He dipped his right hand into his pocket and drew something out—something which glinted in the light; a knife.

Rollison moved from the threshold and stepped just inside the room, taking out his cigarette-case to use as a missile; the knife might be intended only to frighten, and probably was, but it could so easily be used to kill.

Rollison crept forward.

'That's better,' the intruder said. 'Now don't lie to me. Where are they?'

Barbara didn't answer.

The man leaned forward.

'*Where are they?*'

'I—I don't know what you mean!' she gasped.

'So you don't know what I mean,' sneered the man. 'It's time you remembered, sweetie, or I'll rip your guts out. I mean the sparklers.'

'The—sparklers?' she echoed blankly.

The knife flashed in front of her face and she drew back, banging her head on the panel of the bed. She drew a hissing breath. The man's body hid her face now, but Rollison could imagine the terror on it as he went forward. He did not want to act a moment too soon.

'The diamonds, you little slut. Where are they?'

'Di—*diamonds?*' stammered Barbara. 'I don't know what you're talking about! I haven't any diamonds, except these.' She held up her left hand and her engagement ring flashed. 'I don't know——'

The man made another feint with the knife and thrust his other hand over her mouth, to stifle any scream. Rollison didn't speak, just moved quietly over the carpeted floor and, as the intruder began to threaten again, stretched out his right hand and gripped the wrist which held the knife.

The burglar made an incoherent noise in the back of his throat and tried to free his hand, but Rollison's fingers gripped more tightly and he twisted. The knife fell on to the bed. Rollison kept his hold on the man's wrist, and patted his pockets and felt under his arms. He felt no other weapon, so pushed the man aside. His victim stumbled against the bed and fell backwards, legs waving, the lock of hair falling to the sheet. Rollison caught one of his ankles and thrust him vigorously back, over the bed. The man hit the floor with a thud, and the trinkets on the dressing-table shook. The bed-side lamp tottered.

Rollison smiled at Barbara.

'Let's have some more light, will you?'

She slid out of bed and hurried to the main switch, fingering her hair as she went. When the ceiling light came on, the intruder was sitting on the floor, moistening his lips and staring. He had a bullet-shaped head and a very thick neck. His dark hair was cut short, almost in a prison-crop. His broad nose and flat lips were almost negroid, but his skin was white. He was

27

a florid, ugly-looking creature with powerful shoulders and a thick barrel-like torso.

'Get up,' ordered Rollison.

The man didn't move.

'Get—*up*.' Rollison leaned over the bed, bent down and grabbed the man's wrist, pulled him to his feet and gave him a shove against the wall. He came up against it with another thud and nearly fell again. He shot out a hand and clutched the dressing-table for support. The trinkets rattled, a brush fell to the floor.

'I should get back to bed if I were you,' Rollison said to Barbara.

She obeyed; her nightdress was thin and the room cold. She sat down and pulled a blanket round her shoulders, looking first at Rollison and then at the burglar.

'Take off your coat,' Rollison said to the man.

After a short, tense pause, the man did so.

'Throw it on the bed,' ordered Rollison.

Again the man obeyed, and the coat fell on the bed, near Barbara.

'Pick it up, Mrs. Allen, and empty the pockets,' said Rollison, 'We'll see what we can learn about the gentleman.'

He looked into the scared brown eyes of his victim, who moistened his lips again and stood up more comfortably. Barbara began to go through the pockets, but kept looking at the burglar and at Rollison. Oddments piled up on the bed by her side, and Rollison did not speak until every pocket was empty.

A wallet, some letters, a gold watch, a slim gold cigarette-case and a lighter, a piece of billiard-chalk, a green comb, a small ring of keys, a book of stamps and some other oddments came to light.

'Now I wonder where you won the gold watch,' said Rollison, with a touch of mockery. 'The last crib you cracked, I suppose. What's all this about diamonds?'

The man didn't speak.

'I shouldn't hold out on me, chum,' Rollison said mildly. 'The telephone is in the hall, and the police will be here in five minutes if I dial 999. What's all this about diamonds?'

'Why the hell don't you ask *her*?' growled the intruder.

'Because I prefer you to tell me,' said Rollison. Mrs. Allen, pick up that hair-brush and give it to me, will you?' He glanced at the silver hair-brush on the floor and Barbara got off the bed. She looked a comical figure with a blanket clutched round her, one corner trailing on the floor. Instinctively, she looked at herself in the mirror, and felt her hair again.

She picked up the brush.

'Throw it,' said Rollison, and she did so. He caught it deftly by the handle and beat the air with it. 'This is almost as good as a cosh,' he mused aloud. 'You know what a cosh is, don't you chum? A shiny sheath of leather filled with lots of lead shot. On the whole I think this will hurt more. Now what were you saying about those diamonds?'

The man glanced at the brush, as if trying to make up his mind whether Rollison meant to use it—and Rollison darted forward and struck him on the top of the head.

'Just to show you that I mean business,' said Rollison. 'And if you get really awkward, I'll try your knife. Think how much trouble and pain you can save by opening your mouth.'

The man darted a swift glance at Barbara.

'She—she's got them!' he gasped.

'Don't be silly,' said Barbara, as she sat down again.

'She has!' barked the man.

'She has—she hasn't—she has—she hasn't—now there isn't any more fluff on the puff-ball,' said Rollison, his voice hardening. Mrs Allen, whom are those letters addressed to?'

'*Letters?*' Barbara was startled.

'Those you took out of his pocket.'

Barbara picked them up; there were three. The man by the wall looked from Rollison to her and back again as she read.

'They're all addressed to—to Harold Blane,' Barbara said quickly.

'Harold Blane,' echoed Rollison. 'Harold, I am not fooling. I'm going to hear your story before you leave here if I have to break your bones to make you talk. You came here to get some diamonds which you think Mrs Allen keeps in the flat —what makes you think so?'

'They *must* be here,' muttered Blane. 'They must be!'

'Oh, a case of logic, is it?' asked Rollison. 'Some of your boy friends searched the flat this afternoon and found nothing. Others—maybe you were among them—persuaded Bob Allen to take a little ride with you, and you made sure he hadn't got them on him, so—they must be here. Right?'

'You—you *know*,' gasped Blane.

29

'Just a little guess-work, Harold,' said Rollison, and turned to Barbara. 'Ever seen this creature before?'

'I—no, no. He wasn't one of the gas-men.'

'I shouldn't imagine he's a gas-man by profession,' murmured Rollison. 'The question is whether he's one of the same party or whether there are two parties with the same idea.'

He moved again, and caught the burglar's chin between the fork of his finger and thumb and banged his head against the wall. The movement startled Barbara almost as much as the victim, it was so swift and violent. And it was followed by a harsh-voiced:

'*Are* you one of the gas-men's friends?'

'Yes!' gasped the burglar.

'That looks like the set-up, Mrs. Allen,' Rollison said. 'Your husband's supposed to have some diamonds, and some bad men want them. Simple greed, you see. Have you——'

'I've never seen any diamonds!' exclaimed Barbara. 'Bob can't have them!'

'They aren't on Allen,' Blane said. 'They weren't found here this afternoon, so they must——'

'Two things are possible,' interrupted Rollison judicially. 'Either Allen has hidden them in a safe place, or he never had them.'

'He had them all right!'

'As you're so sure, where did he get them from?'

'I—I don't know,' muttered Blane. He drew back, as if frightened of being hurt again. 'I don't know! I was told——'

'Who told you?'

'The Boss!'

'So the Boss told you,' said Rollison, shaking his head. 'When in doubt, invent an all-powerful Boss and blame everything on to him, as with Cabinet Ministers. *Who told you?*'

'It's true!' gasped Blane. 'I've told you the truth, the Boss——'

'Who is this gentleman?'

'*I don't know!*' Blane's voice grew hoarse as Rollison took a step towards him, and raised the hair-brush.

'Well, well, isn't that a remarkable thing,' marvelled Rollison. 'The Boss gives you orders and sends you out with a knife, and knows everything about Bob Allen and the mysterious diamonds, but you don't even know the Boss's name.'

He struck out with the brush.

Blane kicked at his groin, letting fly with all his strength, but Rollison moved again with bewildering speed, grabbed Blane's ankle and thrust his leg aside. Blane crashed—the loudest crash of all.

'You hurt yourself that time,' said Rollison mildly. 'Whichever way you move you're bound to get hurt—one way more badly than another. Now, Harold!'

He yanked the man to his feet, pushed him into an easy chair, and demanded with deceptive gentleness:

'Who sent you here?'

Blane didn't answer, but was desperately frightened now. His lips twitched, he didn't know what to do with his hands.

Barbara broke across his words with a startled cry, Blane glanced towards the door. Rollison backed swiftly away—and saw another man standing on the threshold, gripping a walking stick in his right hand.

CHAPTER FIVE

CURIOUS BEHAVIOUR

'Bob!' cried Barbara, and jumped from the bed, sending Blane's possessions flying about the floor. 'Bob!'

There was anguish in her cry.

It was understandable, Allen's face was bruised and scratched, there was an ugly cut on his forehead, and his clothes were torn. Although his eyes were glittering and he held the walking-stick as if it were a weapon, his mouth was wide open, and he breathed laboriously; he must have held his breath to keep silent while coming across the hall.

'Bob!'

'Keep away!' gasped Allen. 'Don't——'

Blane jumped out of his chair.

'Get me out of here!' he rasped. 'If you don't, you know what's coming to you. Get me out!'

'We've different ideas about that,' said Rollison. 'You stay where you are. Allen, I'm——'

'I don't give a hoot in hell what you are,' growled Allen, motioning to Blane. 'Get out—I'm not stopping you.'

31

'Now, Allen!' began Rollison.

'Bob——' Barbara's voice broke.

Allen glared at his wife and advanced a step into the room, raising the stick threateningly. Blane went towards the door, watching Rollison out of the corner of his eyes. Suddenly he made a dive—for the knife, which was still on the bed. Rollison shot out a hand and pushed him away, then tossed the sheet over the knife.

Blane hesitated, and Allen shouted:

'Get out, you fool!'

'Allen——' began Rollison.

'Shut your mouth!' roared Allen, and when Rollison grabbed at Blane, he struck out with the stick. The carved handle caught Rollison on the shoulder. Barbara cried: 'Bob, don't!' but Allen pushed Rollison aside. Blane paused on the threshold, then turned and disappeared.

The front door slammed.

'Oh, you're mad!' gasped Barbara. 'Bob, you're crazy!'

Allen tossed the stick on to the bed, and limped across to the chair. He sank into it. Perspiration beaded his forehead and his eyes looked glassy. The blood on his face had coagulated and was a dark-brown colour except in one place, where it still welled up a bright crimson. He leaned back, resting his head on the top of the chair, but didn't close his eyes.

He looked at Rollison.

'Bob——' began Barbara.

'For pity's sake, shut up!' muttered Allen. He winced, and pressed a hand against his stomach. He couldn't breathe through his nose. As he looked at Rollison, he seemed to sag, and couldn't meet that unnerving gaze. There was a moment of almost unbearable tension—then Rollison broke it.

'Mrs. Allen, get a bowl of water and a towel.'

'But——'

'Please hurry,' said Rollison.

Barbara shot a glance at her husband, who did not look at her, then went out. Rollison stood a few feet in front of Allen, who looked towards the ceiling, wincing every now and again. Rollison kept silent until Allen cried:

'Who the devil are you?'

'A friend of Snub Higginbottom,' said Rollison promptly.

'Snub's? Did she—send for you?'

32

'For him, but he's away. She's had a rough time.'

'*She's* had a rough time,' gasped Allen. It was nearly a sneer. 'What do you think I've had?'

Rollison said slowly:

'You've had a beating-up, and from what I can see of things, you asked for it, and you've just asked for another.'

Allen said: 'Okay, give me one. *I* can't stop you.'

Defiance and challenge showed in his eyes, in spite of his plight; no one could question his courage. But Rollison's manner changed, the pity faded, contempt replaced it.

They heard water running in the bath-room; something clattered in the bath, loud enough to make Allen jump. Barbara had dropped the bowl.

'Well?' muttered Allen. 'Get your damned questions out.'

'When you let Blane go, you invited another beating-up because he and his friends will come after you again,' said Rollison. 'The police——'

'Keep your damned nose out of my business!' shouted Allen. 'If you go to the police——'

'It *might* save your wife's life,' said Rollison.

That broke Allen's defiance and made him silent.

'It might even save yours,' went on Rollison, 'but I don't think that matters so much. At this rate, you'll continue to make a little hell on earth both for her and for yourself. 'Why were you beaten up to-night?'

'That's my business.'

'Did Blane do it?'

'Maybe he did, maybe he didn't.'

Rollison said gently: 'All right, Allen, have it your own way. The police——'

'You mustn't call the police!' Allen cried. He tried to sit up. 'I'll tell you what I can. It was Blane and two other men. I'd been to the B.B.C.; they were waiting for me when I came out, and made me get into a cab. They—they wanted to know something I couldn't tell them and—and they beat me up. They blind-folded me and took me to a house, and beat me up again, but I convinced them that I couldn't help them——'

He stopped, leaving the sentence in the air.

'And couldn't you?' asked Rollison softly.

'No!'

Barbara came in with the bowl of water and towel.

Rollison took a sheet from the bed and put it round Allen's

shoulders. Barbara went out again and returned with a bottle of antiseptic, another towel, some lint and adhesive plaster.

Together, they worked on Allen's face in silence, cleansing and bathing the cuts. The only serious one was that on the forehead, but Rollison did not think it needed stitching. In a box which Barbara had brought was a tube of zinc ointment, and Rollison spread some on a piece of lint, placed it gently on the long cut, then kept it in place with plaster.

At last the task was done.

Rollison said: 'Now what's the matter with your stomach, Allen.'

Allen muttered: 'A kick, that's all.'

'Better let's have a look at it,' said Rollison.

He helped Allen to undress and lie down on the bed. There were red marks on the skin—'a kick' probably meant several. There were bruises at his waist, too, where the skin was broken in places. Rollison washed the bruises with iodine; then, without speaking, he helped Allen to sit up against the pillows.

'Easier?' he asked.

'I'm all right,' muttered Allen.

'I think a doctor ought to have a look at your midriff,' Rollison said, 'there might be more damage than we can see.'

'I've had a kick in the belly before!' snapped Allen. 'And you've over-stayed your welcome, it's time you went.'

Barbara opened her mouth to speak, but at a glance from Rollison, gathered up the soiled towels and the bowl, and went out without a word. Allen didn't watch her; he seemed to take no interest in her.

'You deaf?' demanded Allen.

'I'm not quite ready to go,' said Rollison, looking up as Barbara returned. 'Could there be hot coffee, with plenty of sugar?' he asked, and she went off again. Rollison pulled the blankets and eiderdown over Allen, then stood by the side of the bed. He lit a cigarette and put it to Allen's mouth.

'Allen,' he said, 'you've scared your wife so much that she hardly knew what she was doing when she asked Snub for help.'

'What do you know about him?' demanded Allen. 'Why did you——'

'He works for me. And he's on holiday.'

'And you're King Arthur,' sneered Allen.

Rollison said: 'Blane might knock his moll about, but he

wouldn't be so viciously cruel as you are to your wife.'

'You needn't read the Riot Act,' growled Allen.

'It's time someone did,' said Rollison. 'You're so full of yourself and your own miserable skin that you haven't even the grace to ask why I'm here, or what made your wife send for Snub. You've been living so long with savages who've looked on you as a god that you've forgotten how to behave in England. It's a pity you ever got back.'

A curious gleam sprang into Allen's eyes.

'Go on, finish it,' he sneered.

'You can finish it yourself,' said Rollison. 'Maybe if you tried to forget your own troubles and think of your wife's, you'd improve, but there doesn't seem much chance of that. She was nearly murdered this afternoon.'

'That's a lie!'

'That's the truth,' said Rollison. 'She was attacked by two friends of Blane—friends of the man you helped to escape. They chloroformed her. But she's so loyal to you that she didn't send for the police because that might come back on you. But I'm not interested in your safety, Allen.'

Allen took the cigarette from his lips, and mocked:

'You seem pretty interested in something.'

'I'm interested in a friend of Snub,' said Rollison. 'Still glad you let Blane go?'

'I—I had to let him go.'

'Because you've lost everything, even the will to make a fight of it,' said Rollison bitingly.

'What's the use of fighting?' asked Allen. He drew on the cigarette again, and stared at the glowing tip. 'You're right, I'm a heel—I told Bar so this morning. She's a fool to stay with me. I didn't know—anything had happened to her, or would happen.'

'You must have known there was a risk.'

'I wouldn't tell her anything, in case the others tried—tried to find out what she knew.'

'You just let her suffer in misery and fear, and hoped for the best. You forgot too many things while you were in Burma. You've got to start learning all over again.'

'Why don't you shut up?' Allen asked wearily. 'I've had a hell of a time. I—I'm sorry about Bar, I thought she'd be all right, but she isn't badly hurt. And Blane had to go.'

Barbara came in, carrying a tray; she had made a jugful of

35

coffee and brought three cups and some biscuits. She put the tray on the bedside table and began to pour out. She put a spoonful of sugar into Allen's cup; Rollison added three more and stirred it slowly.

Since she had entered the room not a word had been spoken, but Allen looked at her, and Rollison read something in his expression which Allen probably didn't know was there.

'Now drink this while it's hot,' Rollison said.

Allen sipped.

Rollison drank also . . .

'Now,' he said briskly, 'you ought to take some aspirins and get a good night's sleep. If your tummy's painful in the morning—more painful that you'd expect from a bruise—send for a doctor. Probably I shall come over myself and give you a once-over,' he added. 'You ought to take some to steady you, too, Mrs. Allen; there won't be any more trouble to-night.'

'How can you be sure of that?' asked Barbara.

'I'll make sure,' said Rollison.

'You mean—you'll send for the police? Please don't——'

Rollison said: 'See, Allen? You just don't deserve it. No, not the police, Mrs. Allen, some other friends of mine. May I use the telephone?'

'Of course,' said Barbara, jumping up, and her eyes were much brighter.

'I know where it is,' said Rollison.

He went out, closing the door behind him.

His last glimpse of the couple then, was of Barbara standing by the side of the bed and Allen, his eyes closed and his face set.

He lifted the telephone and dialled an Aldgate number.

For many years Bill Ebbutt had been a prize-fighter; for many more he had been the owner of the *Blue Dog*, in the Mile End Road. During most of this period he had known Rollison, whom he sometimes called 'Mr. Ar' and sometimes 'The Torf' and occasionally something meaty and to the point. He was inordinately fond of Rollison, who was *persona grata* in Bill's flat above the *Blue Dog*, and also at the gymnasium. Bill was passionately devoted to the fistic art, and it was his dream not only that England should win world championships again, but that the world-beaters should receive their early training 'in the gym'. Ebbutt lavished as much care and attention, devotion and selflessness on the gym and his 'boys' as his wife did on the Salvation Army; and her devotion to that was so great that she had once persuaded Bill to be 'saved'. She had even tried to interest Mr. Ar.

Rollison knew the gymnasium, which was in its way a club, very well. He frequently stepped in for a word with Ebbutt and a bout with a young hope who stroked him gently round the ring, afraid of releasing a real punch, because of Bill's watchful eye.

Although Bill Ebbutt did not keep early hours, he slept heavily, and he was asleep when the telephone bell rang at nearly one o'clock that morning.

His wife did not stir.

The telephone bell kept ringing.

With a gargantuan sigh, Ebbutt heaved his seventeen stone off the massive iron bedstead. He kicked his foot on a chair, swore and crept to the door. The bell kept on and on, sounding much louder when he opened the door.

He crept on to the small landing.

'*William!*' called his wife.

'S'orl right, telephone,' growled Ebbutt.

'Never you mind the telephone,' said Mrs. Ebbutt, 'using language what you ought to be ashamed of in the middle of the night, you ought to be ashamed of——'

'For Pete's sake shut your mouth,' said Ebbutt, with some impatience.

When he reached the hall-passage, the bell stopped. He switched on a light and blinked in the glare, his good humour spent. In a pair of vividly-striped red-and-blue pyjamas, his wispy grey hair standing on end and his calloused feet bare, he was a remarkable sight.

'Come orn, if you're going to,' he growled, and put out his hand to switch off the light. Immediately darkness fell, the bell began to ring again. 'Cor!' he exploded. When at last he lifted the receiver, he barked: ''Oo in perishin' 'ell is it? ... Oo? ... I can't 'ear ... Mr. Ar!' he breathed as if syrup had poured into his mouth. 'Strike a light, I never thought it was you! ... S'orl right, Mr. Ar, I wasn't asleep ... What?'

He listened attentively, closing one eye and staring at the ceiling. He nodded, as if Rollison could see him. He grunted and finally said:

''Ow many? ... Two enough? ... Okay, Mr. Ar, you just

leave it ter me ... sure, right away, I 'eard you say it 'ad to be right away. Take me abaht three-quarters of a n'our—they'll be there all right, Mr. Ar. Anyfink up?'

And what Rollison said then made him shake with gusty laughter.

A little more than three-quarters of an hour later Rollison left Byngham Court Mansions. He had with him all the contents of Blane's pockets and the knife, which was wrapped in a serviette, to preserve the finger-prints.

In the doorway of a house near-by was a shadowy figure, who emerged from the gloom and called to him in a hoarse whisper.

'It's me, Mr. Ar.'

'Hallo, Sam,' greeted Rollison, making out the tall figure of one of Bill's one-time 'white hopes'. 'Nice night, isn't it?'

'Loverly. Any special orders, Mr. Ar?'

'Top landing, Sam. There's a chair outside, I've fixed it, and the people there know you're going to be around. Who's at the back?'

'Bert Dann,' said Sam. 'Bill fought you'd better 'ave a little 'un for the back, 'e can nip up the fire-escape pretty quick.'

'Wonderful!' praised Rollison. 'If the couple in Flat 31 ask for help, get cracking. If nothing happens, Bill's going to send someone to relieve you in the morning. Don't let the police see you if you can help it, but if you get in a jam, blame me for it—that'll get you out!'

'You needn't worry abaht *me,*' declared Sam confidently, 'or abaht Bert, Mr. Ar.'

'I know I needn't,' said Rollison.

He walked to the entrance to the next block of flats, where he had left his *Sunbeam-Talbot.* He drove swiftly through the deserted streets, thinking a little about Bill Ebbutt and his boys, more about Barbara Allen, much about Allen himself—and the diamonds. He had no doubt that they existed, but Allen had refused to admit it, saying that he knew nothing about any precious stones, and had maintained that attitude no matter how Rollison had tried to shift him or his wife cajoled.

Rollison put the car away in a garage near Gresham Terrace, slipped the key into his pocket and walked into the street. A clock struck two. Ebbutt had wasted no time, and if the Allens did get more visitors that night, the visitors would have a rude shock. He hurried up two flights of stairs to his flat, and as he neared the top of the second flight, still thinking about the diamonds, he thought he saw something move.

He missed a step, deliberately.

It was dark up here, but a faint light came from the hall below, where a dim bulb burned all night. He couldn't be sure whether he had seen the movement, but now, as he went up more quietly, he smelt tobacco smoke. He hummed softly, as if he hadn't a suspicion, took his key and slipped it into the lock. Deliberately he fumbled with it. He was sure now that someone moved. He opened the door a few inches but stopped to take the key from the lock—and as he did so something hard was jammed into his ribs and a man hissed:

'Don't make a sound!'

Slowly, Rollison put up his hands.

CHAPTER SIX

WARNING

'KEEP still,' ordered the man behind Rollison. It wasn't Blane; Rollison would have recognised the voice. 'Listen to me, and don't make any mistake about it. Leave the Allens alone.'

'The Allens?' Rollison pretended surprise—in fact, there was not much need to pretend. The 'something' was pressed harder into his ribs.

'You know who I mean,' the man said. It was pitch dark. They were half inside the hall of the flat, and there was no glimmer of light here; the radiance from downstairs didn't spread as far as this. Rollison could feel the man's breath on the back of his neck, so he was tall.

'Keep out of the Allens' affairs, see. You saw Allen tonight, didn't you?'

'Yes. I saw the wreck.'

'That's nothing to what will happen to you if you poke your nose in,' growled the unknown. 'You won't know whether you're coming or going.'

'But I'm,' said Rollison, 'I'm staying here.'

'You'd better stick *right* here,' the man said. 'This is something you can't tackle. It's too big for you or anyone else. You

39

won't help the Allens by going to the police, and you'll only get bashed if you try anything yourself. Got me?'

'You've made it all very clear,' said Rollison.

The man pushed him forward, sending him staggering into the hall, and slammed the door. Rollison came up against the wall as a light went on in Jolly's room, and Jolly's door burst open. Jolly gave the Toff one glance and rushed to the front door, a vision in yellow.

'Careful!' called Rollison.

'I will be, sir.' Jolly opened the door an inch and peered on to the landing 'I don't think——' he began.

The street door slammed.

'You can relax,' said Rollison, moving from the wall and brushing his hair out of his eyes. Dishevelled, there was a ruggedness about him that had not been noticeable before. 'I think he had a gun, but it may have been a bit of wood.'

'Shall I——' began Jolly.

'You will *not* go out the back way and trail him,' said Rollison firmly. 'He's almost certainly haring along the street by now. It's a night for letting bad men get away, so we may as well keep in the fashion. Sorry you were disturbed, Jolly.'

'I'm sorry *you* were roughly handled, sir,' said Jolly.

'He could have been much rougher,' Rollison confided. 'He was waiting on the landing and had one fixed idea. To put the fear of death into me.'

'Then he could not have known you very well,' observed Jolly.

Rollison chuckled.

'Nicely said! On the other hand, he knew me and he knew that I'd been to see the Allens. The position is this: Mrs. Allen is distressed because her husband is in a spot, and he . . .'

There were few gaps left in the story five minutes later, and Jolly, whose ability to grasp quickly the essentials of such a recital was unrivalled, forbore to ask questions, although he looked very thoughtful. He was lukewarm about Ebbutt's men but he accepted them philosophically.

Ten minutes after the door had slammed on Rollison, they went to their rooms. Almost immediately afterwards, Rollison came out of his and went to the front door.

He opened the door, as Jolly called:

'Have I forgotten anything, sir?'

'No, *I* had. A pity the key was in the lock.'

'*Was*, sir?'

'Was.'

'Then I will arrange for a new lock to be put on to-morrow morning,' said Jolly. 'I think that would be wisest, don't you?'

Rollison considered.

'Yes,' he agreed, 'and then again, no. If they've a key and want to get in, why not let them? We could prepare a petting party for prying prodnoses.'

'With respect,' said Jolly, 'I think you have taken too many risks already. The risk with Mrs. Allen and the man Blane was, perhaps, justified, although you would have felt very badly, very badly *indeed*, sir, had Blane been there with the express purpose of murdering Mrs. Allen.'

'I would, but it wasn't likely,' Rollison said.

'It was possible,' said Jolly firmly. 'And I think you were ill-advised to allow this man to hold you up, sir, since you had warning of his presence, he might also have been here with homicidal intent.'

'Pessimistic to-night, aren't you?' asked Rollison.

'I see no reason why you should risk being murdered, sir. There are risks and *risks*.'

'You have a Johnsonian profundity at times,' said Rollison solemnly. Yes, Jolly, I will have a care.'

'Thank you, sir,' said Jolly. 'Good-night again.'

'Good-night,' said Rollison gravely.

Rollison closed his door behind him, smoothed down his hair, exuded a long breath, and sat down on the foot of the bed to take off his shoes. He undressed slowly, thinking of diamonds—chloroform—a terrified man—a distressed wife—a knife—fear of the police—and violent gentlemen who acted with quite remarkable speed. This, then, was no ordinary affair of crime. Of course not. Allen's fear and consequent wildness; his wife's misery; these things were damnable.

He was tired; he must get to sleep, and in the morning bring a clear mind to bear upon events. He was already drowsy, and all was well for to-night. To-morrow——

He slept.

He stirred, because of a sound in the flat. He tried to ignore it, but the sound was too insistent. A bell was ringing.

He woke up reluctantly.

The bell kept ringing.

Bill Ebbutt must have felt something like this when he had

41

been disturbed. Who on earth was calling at this time of the night? The Allens? He flung back the bed-clothes, suddenly wide awake and alarmed. The main telephone was in the hall, and there was an extension to the study, but not to any of the bedrooms. He switched on the bedside light and hurried across the room—and as he opened the door, Jolly entered the hall, blinking.

'Yes, sir,' said Jolly.

Rollison lifted the receiver, now convinced that it was the Allens. He said: 'Rollison speaking,' and heard a sound—as if Button A were being pressed. He was prepared to hear Barbara's voice, not the pleasant, mellow voice of a man.

'Is that Mr. Richard Rollison?'

'Yes, speaking.'

'I'm so sorry to disturb you at this hour,' said the caller, 'but I think it better that you should be disturbed like this than —be hurt, don't you?'

Rollison said slowly: 'I don't quite understand.'

'It's a shame when you're not yet fully awake,' said the other, with a laugh in his voice. 'You remember the man who called to see you about an hour ago?'

Rollison said: 'Vaguely.'

'Oh, it will soon be clearer,' the other assured him. 'I just want you to know that he was serious. I should hate to have any misunderstanding.'

'Oh, there's no fear of that,' said Rollison. 'Which of your boy friends learned my name?'

'I have an envelope addressed to you in my hand this very moment,' said the caller. 'It was in the dashboard pocket of your car. And my messenger remembers—vaguely—what a pity people are vague!—that you have something of a reputation for helping lame dogs over stiles. Allen isn't a lame dog.'

'He's a lame man.'

The other laughed.

'Yes, isn't he? He broke his leg doing something he shouldn't have done, it isn't true that he broke it when his plane crashed. But don't take me too literally and don't be persuaded by an attractive young woman that you ought to become a modern Don Quixote. This is an age of selfishness.'

'You're quite a philosopher,' remarked Rollison.

'I am many things,' said the caller, 'and particularly a man

42

of my word. Don't come into this affair, Mr. Rollison. Be advised. Keep out.'

The sound of the receiver being hung up crackled in Rollison's ear. He turned and contemplated his man, no longer the slightest bit drowsy. The caller's mellow voice had held a quality of menace, not wholly hidden by the note of laughter. According to Barbara, Allen was terrified by a man with such a voice and a man who knew exactly what he aimed to do, and was extremely self-confident.

A sound disturbed Rollison again, the ringing of a bell, at first far away and then much nearer, until it seemed to be almost in his ear. The fumes of sleep receded slightly. Confound it, this was too bad; it was still pitch-dark. Jolly could—no, it wasn't fair on Jolly. He got out of bed. The bell kept ringing. Perhaps the Allens—but he didn't worry about the Allens, Bill's men were there. Good old Sam and Bert.

He reached the telephone.

Jolly spoke from his door, a bleary-eyed figure.

'Can I help, sir?' he asked glumly.

'Sorry about this,' said Rollison, stifling a yawn. 'Hallo, Rollison speaking,' he said into the telephone.

'Oh, Mr. Rollison!' It was a girl—fresh, eager, almost excited. 'That is *the* Mr. Rollison, isn't it?'

'I hope it's the Rollison you want,' said Rollison, signalling wildly; Jolly turned into the study, to listen-in on the call. 'Who is that?'

'My name doesn't matter, Mr. Rollison,' said the girl, 'but a friend of mine spoke to you a little while ago, didn't he? He just asked me to ring up—to tell you not to forget.'

'Oh,' said Rollison heavily. 'Just that?'

'Yes, you won't forget, will you?' asked the girl brightly.

'I shall not forget.'

'I'm *so* glad,' said the girl, 'and I know he'll be delighted. *Good*-night.'

When next Rollison woke, it was daylight. By his side was morning tea, the newspapers and the post. Among the post was a card from Snub Higginbottom, depicting the belles of Blackpool. This focused Rollison's thoughts on the Allens, and he dwelt on the young couple as he bathed, shaved and breakfasted; later when he went into the study to answer urgent

43

correspondence, Jolly followed.

Jolly by day was a funereal figure, partly because of the clothes of convention, partly because his habitual expression was one of unrelieved gloom. This morning, he looked tired; and, consequently, more glum than ever.

'Dark depressed thoughts, Jolly?' asked Rollison. 'Before we have 'em, send a telegram to Snub, will you, and ask him to catch the first train back.'

'The telegram has already been sent, sir,' said Jolly. 'Here is an affair of violence, which might be construed into attempted murder—not an isolated case, but a series of calculated assaults and a man, or men, who appear to work with complete disregard for the law. Do you agree with that assessment of the situation, sir?'

'Yes,' said Rollison, 'but need you be so aggressive about it?'

'I apologise if I appear to be over-emphatic, sir, but the picture you have drawn of Mr. Allen does not show him in a particularly pleasing light. He is not a nice young man.'

'He was,' said Rollison.

'How can you tell that?' challenged Jolly.

'Because Barbara married him,' said Rollison.

'That may be so, sir,' said Jolly, 'but I have known very nice young women marry—*bounders,* sir. We have no real information about Mr. Allen, and yet we are considering humouring him by withholding information about these crimes from the police. That is a serious offence, sir.'

'Very,' agreed Rollison.

'And unwise, indiscreet, capable of being misunderstood, and possibly leading to considerable disunity between you, and the police,' said Jolly. 'My opinion, sir, is that neither Mr. Allen nor Mrs. Allen is worth taking such risks for.'

'Oh,' murmured Rollison blankly.

'Further, sir,' continued Jolly remorselessly, 'we have obtained assistance from Mr. Ebbutt and some of his friends. You know that Mr. Ebbutt's friends are not always reliable, in so far as they allow their natural exuberance and aggressiveness to override considerations of diplomacy, and they are not alway *persona grata* with the police. It is quite possible that the police will discover that they are taking sides in an affair of violence at your request. If that were to happen, possibly something more grave would follow.'

'Jolly,' said Rollison, 'I quite agree.'

'Then may I hope you—we will advise the police immediately?' asked Jolly.

'No,' said Rollison.

'I hope we won't regret it, sir.'

'But we will protect our flanks,' said Rollison, obligingly. 'Have you seen the oddments I brought back from the Allens last night?'

'Yes, sir, I have seen them—as well as the knife which was wrapped in a table-napkin. I have not touched the handle.'

'Good. You can spend an interesting morning pretending to be a detective,' said Rollison. 'Test that handle for prints, photograph any prints you find, run through the contents of the pockets, find out if there's anything to show us for whom Blane works. Summarise the details on a single sheet of paper, type-written for preference, and have them ready by midday.'

'Very good, sir,' said Jolly. 'You will be going out this morning?'

'Yes. I'm going to find out all that I can about young Allen —what he was before the war, what really happened to him in Burma, whether he's interested in precious stones, whether events have made him what he is to-day. All these and other things, Jolly, including—why was he asked to broadcast in *In Town To-night*?'

'Many people who appear fleetingly in the public eye broadcast in that programme, sir,' remarked Jolly.

'Oh, yes. But Allen's been home for several weeks. The B.B.C., whatever may be its shortcomings, is never weeks behind with the news. Allen was news a little while ago—I dimly remember reading something about him in the *Morning Cry*— but he isn't news now. Yet suddenly the B.B.C. wakes up to the fact that he has a story which will probably interest the three or four million listeners who switch on at 6.15 every Saturday night.'

'Ten million, I understand,' corrected Jolly dimly.

'Well, all the great British public doesn't want the Third Programme,' remarked Rollison, 'we can't all be like you, Jolly. Anything else?'

'I *would* like to ask one further question, sir, if I may.'

'You may.'

'*Why* do you think it unnecessary to inform the police of what has been happening?' pleaded Jolly. 'It occurs to me that you must have some special reason.'

'I have,' said Rollison, quietly. 'The look in Barbara Allen's eyes.'

Rollison was still thoughtful when he dialled a Mayfair number. Soon an old friend, named Wardle, was on the line. His voice portrayed the man—a well-modulated B.B.C. voice from which one deduced striped trousers and a black jacket.

'Hallo, Rolly,' said Wardle, 'what are you up to now? You wouldn't telephone me at this hour of the morning unless you wanted something.'

'I do. Information about *In Town To-night.*'

'Want to broadcast?' inquired Wardle.

'Heaven forbid!' shuddered Rollison. 'I'm interested in the way the show works—how they pick on the people in town, all that kind of thing. Can you take me along to Broadcasting House and let me have a word with——'

'*In Town To-night* is done from Aeolian Hall,' interrupted Wardle, with the tone of a man who knew that he was talking to an ignoramus. 'I can't manage it this morning or early this afternoon. Conferences. About five o'clock this evening, if I can—I assume that it isn't just idle curiosity?'

'Oh, no. Real live interest. Five o'clock, then, at the Aeolian. Thanks Freddie.'

'Pleasure,' said Wardle. 'Good-bye.'

At half-past eleven that morning Rollison turned his M.G. towards the East End. He drove through the hustle of the West End and the comparative calm of the City, reached Aldgate and, in the space of a few yards, moved from one world to another. Gone were the tall, grey, sombre buildings and the polished brass plates and frosted glass windows, gone were commissionaires and porters in top-hats, those last relics of the days of Dickens, gone were the pale-faced juniors hurrying about their masters' business, and the middle-aged and elderly men who appeared to carry the weight of the world on their shoulders. In their place were the ordinary, humble, humdrum people of the East End. Costers, gentiles, Jews, dark skins and white, barrows, touts outside the windows of the fur *salons,* clattering trams, rows upon rows of little shops.

At a traffic block at the junction of the Mile End Road and Whitechapel Road Rollison first really noticed the taxi with one blue painted wing and one black. He noticed it partly because he was thinking of taxis that morning, and partly because the driver had paused, further back, for an altercation with the chauffeur of a Rolls-Royce. That incident had taken place near St. Paul's, and the taxi was still only a little way behind him.

He kept an eye on it in the driving mirror as he drove along the Mile End Road.

He had dug into Allen's past, largely because he knew an official at the Air Ministry who remembered a great deal about Allen since he had become a sensation.

Allen's record in the R.A.F. had been exemplary; his promotion rapid—and not just because of the war-time gaps made in the ranks of the Wincos. He had been on a special mission when he had been lost. Allen, according to Rollison's informant had combined steadiness with dare-devilry; absolutely nothing was known against him. He had a flair for the theatre and had been in several R.A.F. shows.

Rollison's next call had been to the offices of the *Morning Cry* in Fleet Street, because he remembered that the *Morning Cry* had starred the story of the man who had returned from the dead. Also, he knew Barry Grey, the oldest reporter on the staff—perhaps also the oldest, and certainly the most knowledgeable in Fleet Street. Barry had written up Allen's story, and Rollison had left the office with a firm impression of a steady, likeable young man. Apparently Allen was an architect; his hobby had been amateur theatricals; he was thirty-one; he had been educated at one of the lesser public schools and his father was a clergyman. The amount of irrelevant information which the *Morning Cry* reporter had unearthed and remembered was astonishing, and Rollison felt that he knew everything he needed to know about Bob Allen.

He felt sure now, that Allen had never dealt in precious stones, and had never been wealthy enough to own a collection of them. If Blane had told the truth when he spoke of diamonds, that meant that Allen's interest in them had been comparatively recent.

Rollison drew near a huge cinema which stood out above the low buildings on either side, and looked clean and fresh against the drabness of this part of East London. Near it was a public house which hadn't been painted for decades—but above the front door was fastened a newly-painted sign.

Rollison did not turn into the street near-by, but went on a few hundred yards at a slow pace. Except for two rattling trams, there was no other traffic apart from the M.G. and the taxi with the odd-coloured wings. Rollison kept peering out of the window, as if he had lost his way, and then suddenly swung across the bows of the taxi. The driver braked and bellowed. The solitary passenger was thrown forward and Rollison caught sight of an attractive young woman.

He remembered the voice of the woman who had telephoned him.

When he reached the corner of Derrick Street, where the gymnasium was situated, the taxi was turning round in the main road.

Rollison went on, apparently oblivious, to Bill Ebbutt's gymnasium, behind the Blue Dog.

He left the car outside and, watched by two old men sucking at clay pipes, went into the gloomy interior. The only light was in a corner, where a boxing ring was fitted up. Half a dozen men in short pants and singlets were watching a bout, two or three were doing peculiar and violent things with parallel bars and skipping-ropes.

Leaning against a corner post was the mountainous figure of Bill Ebbutt. The light shone on a cauliflower ear, a broad, flat nose and part of his bull-shaped neck. Bill was as nearly shapeless as a human being could be. His coat was too long, reaching half-way down his thighs, and he wore a white choker.

He did not look round as Rollison approached, but occasionally called out in a squeaky voice:

'Use yer right—what yer gotta left for—feet, you elephants, use yer feet.'

These, and sundry other comments, came with split-second timing.

Rollison stood behind Ebbutt and watched the boxers. One was an old, battered, hairy prize-fighter, like Sam. The other was young, powerful, white-skinned, with little or no hair on his chest; the little was golden. This young man boxed with fierce determination and was getting the better of his hit-and-hope opponent.

At last, Ebbutt bellowed: 'Stop!'

The boxers dropped their hands as if they were worked by machines, and Bill, climbing laboriously into the ring, took hold of the young man's arm and lectured him in a voice which carried to every corner of the huge room. Soon the discomfited youth slunk off to the dressing-room, accompanied by

48

his sparring partner.

Ebbutt squeezed through the rope and picked up a bottle of beer which stood in the corner. He drank from the bottle. And as he drank and, consequently squinted, he caught sight of Rollison. He spluttered, coughed, snatched the bottle away and, having considerable difficulty with his larynx, approached him.

'You mighta told me——' he began reproachfully.

'I was watching the youngster. Useful, isn't he?'

Bill lowered his voice to a confidential whisper and looked across at the dressing-rooms.

'Useful!' he said. 'That boy's a world-beater. Got a punch that will knock Joe Louis silly. S'trew. But never mind that now, Mr. Ar, 'ow *are* you?'

And he extended a massive hand.

Rollison shook it warmly.

'I'm all right, Bill—and getting about a bit again. Your fellows have had a dull time at Byngham Court Mansions, I'm afraid, but things might wake up.'

'Dunno that I want 'em to,' said Ebbutt, sagely, 'big believer in bluff, I am—you know me. Put a coupla toughs outside the flat an' anyone who comes rahnd looking for trouble, beats it. You know me.'

'My good luck,' said Rollison.

'What's it all abaht, Mr. Ar?' asked Ebbutt.

'A young couple are having a rough time but are scared stiff of asking help from the police. I won't let it go too far, and if the situation gets out of hand, tell your boys to call the police.'

'Dunno that they want anyfink to do with the busies,' said Bill, frowning, 'But Okay, Mr. Ar.'

'And I'll tell you the whole story one day,' promised Rollison. 'Bill.'

'Ess?'

'Is Perky Lowe still about?'

'Cor strike a perishin' light, o' course 'e is. On arternoon and evenin' shift. If yer want him yer'll probably find 'im in the *Blue Dog*. But 'e may be at the *Crown*, always shiftin' arahnd, Perky is. Makes a fortune aht've that cab, 'e does. Bought 'is own, did yer know?'

'I didn't. I haven't time to see him now, Bill, but if he can be at Gresham Terrace—near the Piccadilly corner—by one o'clock, I might find him useful.'

'Call it done,' said Bill. 'You know me.'

'That's wonderful,' said Rollison. 'The man who never fails.'

He regretfully refused to go into the *Blue Dog* and have one, inquired after Bill's wife, listened patiently to a story about the Salvation Army, and went out, watched by the same two little old men sucking clay pipes.

The taxi was round the corner, in the main road, and it followed him back to the West End.

Rollison parked his car near *Blott's,* in Coventry Street, and the girl paid off the taxi and went into the famous restaurant some five minutes after him.

CHAPTER SEVEN

BRIGHT YOUNG LADY

SHE sat at a table near him, so that he could only see her profile, and was given prompt and eager attention. She wore a bottle-green suit with a long coat, and a wide-brimmed, white hat with the curling brim swept upwards off her face and cherries glistening on the crown. Her hair was golden in colour and, even in the comparative gloom that was *Blotts* in time of austerity, the lights shone in her hair and her eyes were bright.

A cluster diamond ring sparkled on her engagement finger, a diamond clasp was at the neck of her white blouse. Her gloves and handbag and her shoes were white, and she had most attractive ankles.

Rollison studied the menu.

'If I were you, Mr. Rollison,' murmured the headwaiter, 'I would try the game pie to-day.'

'Game pie,' said Rollison, and considered. 'Henri, I think you're right.'

'Thank you,' said Henri, whose accent suggested that his name should be spelt Henry. 'We haven't had the pleasure of seeing you here for some little time.'

'I've been out of town,' said Rollison. 'Henri.'

'Sir?'

'The young lady on my left.'

Henri's eyes twinkled.

'Yes, Mr. Rollison.'

'How well do you know her?'

'To the best of my knowledge I have never seen her before,' said Henri.

'Oh,' said Rollison, 'that's a pity.'

'It would perhaps be possible for me to tell her that her table has been reserved, it was a mistake to put her* there, to ask her if she would object to sharing a table, perhaps?' Henri had known Rollison for a long time.

'I don't think so,' said Rollison. 'We mustn't rush things.'

'You are the judge, Mr. Rollison.'

'You remember, a few years ago, that I left here by the staff door,' said Rollison hopefully.

'You have done so on more than one occasion,' said Henri.

'And shall again, to-day. This is a conspiracy, Henri. I would like you to give me the swiftest possible service, but cause a series of minor mishaps to happen with the young lady. Her soup—or is it *hors-d'oeuvres?*—could be spilt, perhaps. She could be brought the wrong *entree*—or is it roast? I want to be out at least twenty minutes before she's finished.'

'It shall be done,' said Henri.

From *Blott's* to Gresham Terrace was only a three minute drive. Five minutes after he had slipped out of the staff exit of the restaurant, Rollison entered the hall of the Gresham Terrace flat and called: 'Jolly!' Jolly appeared.

'Sports jacket, flannels, brown shoes, pretend I'm going to Lords,' said Rollison. 'I've got ten minutes.'

'At once, sir!'

Rollison disappeared into the bath-room and took from the cabinet a small box of theatrical make-up. It did not contain everything theatrically necessary, and a star would not have been pleased with the curious assortment of grease-paints, spirit, brushes and accessories—and would have been puzzled by the number of false moustaches and false beards. Rollison eschewed grease-paint, but smeared spirit gum on a small moustache and a Van Dyck beard. As he did this, peering closely into the mirror, Jolly came in. In ten minutes, Rollison was changed; and although no one who knew him well could have been deceived, the beard and moustache made a marked difference to his appearance. He took a pair of black cotton

51

gloves from his wardrobe, tucked them into his pocket and glanced at himself in the mirror.

'Will I do?' he asked Jolly.

'That will suit your purpose, I have no doubt, sir.'

'Good! I'm leaving the car in Leicester Square, fetch it for me in twenty minutes or so.'

'Very good, sir. May I inquire——'

'The young woman who telephoned at four o'clock last night has been following me about all the morning,' said Rollison. 'I am now going to follow her. Any word from Mr. Wardle?'

'He will be happy to meet you at the Aeolian Hall at 5 o'clock this evening, sir.'

'Good,' said Rollison, and went out.

Rollison sat in the taxi, near *Blott's*, and watched the restaurant door. There was a possibility that the girl had already left; there was no way of telling without going into the restaurant, and he did not want to do that. So he smoked a cigarette and chatted with Perky Lowe. Perky, who had helped him before, was a short man with a huge, turnip-shaped head, on the back of which he wore a green cap, as a kind of halo. His eyes were merry and his manner bright. He had a snub nose and discoloured teeth, and smoked continually.

'How's business, Perky?' asked Rollison.

'Pretty good, considering,' said Perky. 'Cor strike a light, I never thought I'd see the day when torfs argued wiv each other for the priv'ledge of riding in my cab!'

'It's a nice change for you,' said Rollison.

'Gets a laugh out of it, I do,' said Perky. 'People ain't arf perlite, too, and they don't tip thruppence no more. They crosses me palm wiv silver, as if I was a ruddy fortune-teller. Know where we're going,' Mr. Ar?'

'I may send you off on your own a bit later on,' said Rollison.

'Well, *I* won't get lorst,' said Perky with a vast grin. 'An' I've got me spanner.'

He had an encyclopaedic knowledge of London and it was his boast that he knew the name and position of every road, street, mews, square and block of buildings in the City, West End and near suburbs.

Rollison had given his instructions when the girl came out of *Blott's* and stood looking up and down, obviously not pleased with herself.

52

'There she is,' said Rollison. 'Don't lose her.'

'Bit of an eyeful,' approved Perky.

The girl turned left and walked along Coventry Street, and the driver moved off as soon as she had gone a dozen yards. She kept looking round, as if hoping to find a free taxi, and actually put her hand up as Rollison's passed. Perky backed into Wardour Street and then invented a little trouble with his engine. The girl walked past, still hailing taxis; opposite the Warner Theatre, she was lucky.

'Now we can move,' said Rollison.

'Okay!' breathed Perky.

His was a newish cab; the girl's an old one which made a circuit of Leicester Square and then returned along Coventry Street and went along Piccadilly. Near New Bond Street, it turned right, took another turning and then swung into a narrow cul-de-sac. Rollison's taxi went past.

'Dead end, sir,' said Perky. 'Lilley Mews, this is,'

'Stay as near as you can, will you?' asked Rollison.

He got out and walked briskly towards the mews. The girl had paid off her taxi and it was swinging round. She disappeared into the doorway of a dingy-looking building. In fact, all the buildings here were dingy, except a garage which had a bright coat of green paint. There were several lock-up garages, but other buildings—which had once been stables—had been turned into flats or houses.

Rollison went first to the garage, but luckily no one came to attend him. He stepped from the garage to the doorway through which the girl had disappeared. On a small plate fastened to the door were the names: *Miss Pauline Dexter—Flat 1. Mr. Oliver Merino—Flat 2.*

The door stood ajar.

Rollison pushed it open and looked into a narrow passage. Facing the door was a short flight of stairs and at the top of that, a freshly painted red door on which was the white numeral, 1. The stairs went higher, with iron railings protecting them; the door of Flat 2 was immediately above that of Flat 1.

He examined the lock of the lower flat, smiled because the tenant doubtless thought it was burglar-proof, then left the building and went back to the garage. A small man with long, greasy hair and long, blackened nails and dirty overalls came out and looked at him with disfavour. Rollison asked if there was a garage available for the night. The garage-hand said no, there wasn't, and didn't add that he was sorry. Rollison asked if he could recommend a garage and the garage-hand said no, he couldn't, and did not appear to be upset about that. Rollison said it was a pity, and a pound note appeared in his right hand. The other pushed his fingers through his hair, to get it out of his eyes, and said:

'Wait a minute, I might be able to fix sunning.'

He returned after five minutes and said that Number 5 was empty for three nights, only for three nights, but number 9 *might* be empty after that. Thirty shillings a week and they were lock-ups. Rollison added thirty shillings to the pound which had already changed hands, and inspected garage number 5. It was spacious and empty, except for an old tyre and one or two dented cans, but what interested Rollison was the fact that it had a small window, about head-high, fitted with plain glass. From the window he could see the doorway through which the girl had gone.

'Yes,' he said, 'this will do nicely.'

'Ain't a better in London,' said the garage-hand. He handed over a bent key, and disappeared.

Rollison turned away, just as the girl came out of the doorway into which she had disappeared.

With her was a tall man of striking appearance, who—and Rollison's eyes crinkled in a smile at the sight—had a fine, neatly trimmed, black beard. He was massive, had a prominent nose, a fine, full mouth and square chin, and he walked with easy grace. He was dressed in a light brown suit of American cut, and wore a wide-brimmed, beige-coloured felt hat—a Stetson, no less. The girl talked to him briskly as they walked towards one of the garages, and the man opened the door with a key. Rollison strained his ears to catch what she said, but succeeded only in hearing odd snatches.

They went into the garage, which was two removed from number 5; car doors slammed, an engine purred, and a minute later a luxurious cream Chrysler nosed into the mews.There was just room for the car to turn; the driver, the man, judged it to a nicety.

Rollison walked after the car rapidly. It was held up at the end of the mews by passing traffic, and Rollison reached Perky's cab before it had gone far.

'I'm not coming with you,' said Rollison. 'Follow that Chrysler, and let me know where it goes. Don't fall down on the job, Perky.'

'What, me?' said Perky. '*You* be careful, Mr. Ar!' He grinned and drove off.

Rollison remembered that cheery grin and the warning, an echo of Jolly's. And he was about to take a risk which nothing could fully justify. He went back to the mews, where the garage remained deserted, and walked boldly to number 7. He did not know which flat the couple had come from; he did not even know whether anyone else was in the flats. So he rang the bell at number 1. There was no answer. He tried again without getting a response, then went upstairs. He opened the letter-box and listened, but heard nothing.

He put on the gloves and then took a knife from his pocket.

It was, in many ways, a remarkable knife, and he had taken it from a remarkable young man who, over a period of years, had cracked crib after crib and remained free of the police. The young man had eventually slipped up and was now languishing on the Isle of Wight, in a prison in a forest. His knife had better fortune. Among its blades there was a long one of flexible steel. Rollison pushed the blade between the door and the lock. The steel, coming up against the barrel of the lock, crept slowly round it and, when the pressure was as strong beyond the barrel as it was on Rollison's side, the lock clicked back. It moved easily, as if it had been recently oiled.

Rollison pushed open the door.

He entered an L-shaped passage, off which five doors led. Two were ajar, three closed. He closed the front door and stood quite still, listening for the slightest sound. It was usually possible to tell whether a room or a flat was occupied—something one sensed without seeing or hearing anything clearly. Nothing suggested that anyone was here. He looked into the rooms where the doors were ajar and found that one was a bath-room and the other the kitchen. On the draining-board were some cups and saucers, plates and dirty knives and forks.

He tried the nearest of the closed doors. This led into a small, luxuriously furnished bedroom with a colour-scheme of primrose and green; a woman's room. The furniture was of bleached oak, and everything had a touch of opulence, contrasting oddly with the dingy exterior of the house.

There were some modern pictures on the walls, and he glanced at the nearest—and widened his eyes when Rollison saw the unmistakable art and signature of Picasso; the owner

55

was a man who spent prodigiously on art. He left the room and tried the next, made sure that no one was in there, and looked into the third. This was the largest of them all, and ran the whole length of the house. There were windows at each end, and the room itself was a drawing-room which would have graced many a country house. The touch of luxury was very evident here; also the thick pile of the beige and red carpet, the soft silken cushions of the same colour, the Bergère suite, the walnut grand piano. The pictures here were water-colours—not particularly modern. There was a Birket Foster, a Wimperis and several others by artists of repute.

On a small table between two chairs were liqueur glasses and on an ash-tray near them, several cigarette-ends. Two were plain, two were red-tipped. So the man—presumably Oliver Merino—and the girl, had sat here. Rollison touched one of the ends, which was quite cold although damp, but another, burned right down after it had been put into the tray, was slightly warm, and there was a faint smell of tobacco smoke.

They had been here not many minutes ago.

'Sorry, Jolly,' said Rollison aloud, and walked across to a fine walnut escritoire, with beautifully carved legs and edges. He pulled at the drawers; every one was locked. He took out the knife again, selected a 'blade' which was in fact a skeleton key, and very soon the drawers were open. Each drawer was neat and tidy; in one were account-books, in another, files of letters, in a third, pens, pencils and stationery. He looked through the account-books which told him little except that there were few accounts noted there, but the few were all large ones. They were curiously kept, too. Instead of having the name and address of the 'customer', each page was headed by letters and numerals. A—A-1—A-2 and so on. Some of the totals of the accounts ran into five figures, none was less than four figures.

He glanced through the letters.

All were addressed to Merino—except a few, which began: *'Dear Oliver.'* The signatures were usually full, not just Christian names. Most of the letters came from abroad—there were several from Paris and New York, some were from Johannesburg, two came from Buenos Aires, one from Lahore, another from Rangoon. The Rangoon letter particularly interested Rollison, simply because it came from Burma. It was brief and to the point:

'Dear Mr. Oliver,

The goods have been despatched by air mail and should reach you about the same time as this. I have no further information about the other matter—I do not think you will get further information from here, they have moved to London all right.

Yours sincerely,
Maurice Fenton.'

And in a circle drawn at the corner of the letter was the cipher: B-2.

Rollison looked at the page in the account-book under that heading—and his lips rounded in an 'O' of astonishment. It was the largest account he had yet seen, and ran into the three hundred thousands. There were thirteen entries, the lowest a total of £11,350. Here and there a single word, such as 'rubies' or 'pearls', suggested that some of the merchandise was jewels.

He replaced the letters and the books and then, with the help of his skeleton key, re-locked the drawers. That done, he looked about the room, wondering where the safe was kept. A wall-safe? Or one let into the floor? Certainly there was no piece of furniture which looked as if it concealed a safe.

He moved the pictures aside, one after the other and when he looked behind the Birket Foster, he found what he sought. Here was a wall-safe, an ordinary combination type with a small knob in the middle of the circular piece of shiny steel. He touched the knob gingerly with his finger—and snatched it away as pain shot through his hand. The safe was electrically controlled—and alive. He rubbed his finger and waited until the stinging sensation had gone, then turned away. If Merino thought the safe worth such protection, it probably contained something very valuable—perhaps the explanation of the big figures in the account-books.

He thought much about Blane and his talk of diamonds.

He went into the kitchen and searched under the sink and in the larder for the electric meter and main switch; he found none. Nor were they in the hall or in the bath-room. He went into the dining-room and bedroom, and could not find what he wanted. He had seen nothing which might conceal a meter in the drawing-room either, but there *must* be a meter.

It might be somewhere outside.

There was no back entrance.

He did not find what he wanted on the narrow landing or anywhere on the stairs.

He returned to Merino's flat, and as he closed the door, he murmured aloud:

'That's very odd—eh, Jolly?' He smiled when he thought of Jolly's reaction to such an impasse as this, then put the thought out of his mind. In the drawing-room, he thought he heard a slight sound and stood still, looking at the windows, seeing garage doors and the drab cobblestones in the roadway. The sound wasn't repeated, it had probably come from outside. He went to the safe again, then tried to trace the electric wiring from that—it might be connected to the mains hidden in the wall; whoever owned this flat would not like to see the untidy contraptions of meter and fuse box in the open. But the wiring was chased, the channel was plastered and painted over.

Then something crashed behind him, and he swung round.

'*Seen enough, mister*?' asked a man.

It was Blane, his head and shoulders above a hole in the floor. He had an automatic in his right hand.

CHAPTER EIGHT

TWO-IN-ONE

BLANE did not appear to recognise Rollison; he had only seen him for a little while and then in electric light. The disguise might be good enough to fool him, although he would need all his wits and a modicum of luck to get away from here.

Behind Blane was a piece of flooring, pushed up from a hinge and resting against the wall that had caused the crash. He was obviously standing on some steps which led from Miss Dexter's, below.

Blane rested his left hand on the floor and came up another step; the gun in his right hand didn't waver.

'Well, have you?' he demanded.

Rollison spoke in a high-pitched, almost falsetto voice.

'I—I'm waiting for Mr. Merino.'

'You're waiting for me, although you didn't know it' Blane came up another step, but he would have to mount at least two more. When he climbed into the room he would be off his balance.

Rollison stood with his mouth gaping and his hands raised as if in sudden fear.

'Get away from the safe,' ordered Blane, and came another step up. 'And don't try any tricks.'

'Tricks?' squeaked Rollison, moving forward. Between him and Blane was a footstool—a little nearer Blane than it was to him.

'Stand still!' snapped Blane.

'But you said——' began Rollison.

He dived forward, grabbed at the stool held it for a fraction of a second and heaved it as Blane fired; the shot rang out, but the bullet missed. The footstool struck Blane in the stomach, and Rollison managed to spring forward from his knees and hands. As he clutched Blane's right wrist, another shot hit the ceiling; then the gun dropped.

'You——' gasped Blane.

Rollison hit him powerfully on the side of the jaw, then struck again. Blane's eyes rolled. He slipped off the ladder and would have fallen, had Rollison not held his arm.

Rollison picked up the gun and brought the butt down on the side of Blane's head, hard enough to knock him out.

He dragged him out of the hole, and across the room, on the alert lest the shots had been heard.

When he was in the doorway, with Blane at his feet, he paused and listened, but heard only a car starting up in the mews. He turned into the kitchen and opened the first drawer, finding what he wanted—a piece of parcel string. He hurried back, tied Blane's hands and feet tightly, stuffed his own handkerchief into the man's mouth, then dragged him into the kitchen and locked the door.

He slipped the key into his pocket and went into the drawing-room, tidying his hair, breathing heavily. Very soon he stood at the bottom of a flight of wooden steps. They led to a small passage, where there was only one door which led into another well-furnished drawing-room. It was not unlike the room upstairs—but smaller, because the little passage was taken out of it. He stepped inside and closed the door. It fitted flush with the wall, and the outline of the door was almost lost in the pattern of the wall-paper—modernist stuff with a series of straight lines and zig-zags. On the walls were large, framed photographs, in colour, of film stars.

He went to the front door of the flat, shot the bolts, then looked for the electric switch. He found it in the kitchen; this one must serve the two flats; Miss Pauline Dexter and Mr. Oliver Merino were doubtless on the best of terms. He switched off the current, then hurried up the ladder to the larger room.

The knob no longer stung him when he touched it.

He might find the right combination quickly; equally it might take him an hour or much longer. He turned the handle right and left, and could just hear the tumblers falling. He did not try any particular combination for a few minutes, but got the feel of the knob and discovered the best angle for hearing the tumblers.

After ten minutes, he gave it up, and stood close to the wall, looking out of the window, feeling disappointed, and yet aware that he had learned much. Now, he faced unpleasant facts. He could keep turning the knob for hours without hitting on the right combination. He might find tools in the kitchen with which he could get at the safe through the wall, but that would take too long.

Better to search through the girl's flat and see what he could find there.

The drawing-room held little of interest—except the photographs. Film stars had autographed these pictures, they were not just printed signatures; here the ink had smudged, there a pen had scratched the smooth surface. Some of the most famous English film stars were there, and all had 'deared' Pauline or been otherwise affectionate.

The small writing-bureau was unlocked. Inside the top drawer was a memorandum pad and a desk diary. Rollison looked through the diary, and an entry for Saturday caught his eye. It said simply 'Aeolian Hall, 3.45 p.m.'

'So she's going there on Saturday, too,' mused Rollison. 'But *In Town To-night* doesn't start until six-fifteen.'

He went into the next room, expecting to find a dining-room.

Instead, it was very like a dressing-room back-stage. There was a long, gilt-framed mirror along one wall and a bench beneath it. Grease-paints and make-up material were spread out on the bench, with two bowls of red roses, one in bud, one in full flower. Inside a wardrobe with sliding doors were several costumes, some modern, some old-fashioned. There were wigs, powders, dozens of pairs of shoes and, in one section, hat was piled upon hat. The other two walls were adorned with more photographs of film stars, some famous, some much less well-known; all of them had signed themselves as if they were on intimate terms with Pauline Dexter, of whom Rollison had never heard.

In a waist-high cupboard, made of the same polished walnut as the wardrobe and the bench, were sheaves of papers—film scripts and one or two B.B.C. scripts. There was some correspondence, too, from the *Meritor Motion Picture Company*. He glanced through it and learned that Pauline Dexter was in the running for a leading part in a film shortly to go on the floor.

He found nothing else of interest, so took another look round the upstairs flat, but added no more to his meagre knowledge of Merino. He looked into the kitchen, where Blane started to struggle as soon as the door was open. So he was all right. Rollison walked quickly past the garage, where the garage-hand was bending over a small car.

He reached Gresham Terrace just after four o'clock, took off the beard and moustache and washed briskly. Then, looking and feeling more himself, he invited Jolly to take tea with him.

Jolly, recognising that as an olive branch, politely accepted.

'Shall I pour out, sir?' he asked.

'Yes,' said Rollison.

'Jolly, I've had a full afternoon and done a great number of things that I shouldn't have done, and I also arranged for Perky Lowe to follow a cream Chrysler about London. Ask him to call back if he comes while I'm out, but get his story.'

'Very good, sir.'

'And we now know that a Mr. Merino, a cream-coloured Chrysler and a film starlet named Pauline Dexter—do you know Pauline Dexter?—are concerned. Have you ever heard of a Mr. Merino?' Rollison added.

Jolly considered.

'I only know the name in connection with wool, sir.'

'Wool?'

'Used, I believe, in the manufacture of underwear,' remarked Jolly. 'A sandwich, sir?'

'Thanks. I seriously doubt if there's any connection between my Merino and underwear. Did you do all those jobs I asked about this morning?'

'Yes, sir.'

'Get any good prints from the knife?'

'Very good ones, sir, and the photographs will be ready some

61

time this evening.'

'Wonderful! As a reward, here's another job. Get hold of Miss Caroline Lawley's maid—do you know her?'

'Slightly, sir,' confessed Jolly.

'And find out from her if she's ever heard of a man named Merino in the motion-picture business. He's a handsome beggar with a swashbuckling air and a black beard which matches his hair and eyebrows, but all might be false. He wears clothes of American cut and likes Stetsons. Also—quite casually if you can—find out what you can about Pauline Dexter, who seems to be under contract to the *Meritor Motion Picture Company*. Miss Lawley's maid is almost certain to know a little bit about Pauline, even if the man Merino is unknown in the film world. Any news from Snub?' he added.

'A telegram, sir, saying that he hoped to be here by seven o'clock,' Jolly said.

'The Allens?'

'I telephoned twice this morning and once this afternoon, and understand that Mr. Allen is in bed and that Mrs. Allen hasn't been out to-day. Sam Willis also telephoned, to say that nothing had happened—he seemed a little disappointed, sir.'

'That shouldn't surprise you,' said Rollison. He finished his tea. 'I must be at the Aeolian Hall at five o'clock,' he added. 'When Mr. Wardle and I have finished a grand tour, I should know more about *In Town To-night* than I do now, and perhaps more about the mystery.'

'And what time will you be back, sir?' asked Jolly.

'I don't know, but I'll dine out.'

He broke off, as the front door bell rang.

Jolly got up and went out. Rollison filled his cigarette case from a box on the desk, and listened to the conversation after Jolly had opened the door.

'Is this the home of Mr. Rollison?' asked a man with a deep voice.

'Yes, sir.'

'And is Mr. Rollison in?'

'I'm not quite sure, sir,' said Jolly. Were he not sure that Rollison should see this man, he would have answered with an emphatic 'no', because he knew how eager Rollison was to leave for the B.B.C. 'If you will please come in, I will find out.'

'Thank you.' The man's voice held a hint of laughter.

'Your name, sir, please?'

'Just say a friend,' said the owner of the deep voice.

Jolly did not press the point but came towards the study. Rollison, already sure who the visitor was, saw him as Jolly pushed the door wider open.

It was Mr. Merino.

CHAPTER NINE

MERINO

'Yes, Jolly,' said Rollison, 'I can spare a few minutes.

'Very good, sir.'

Merino had made no attempt to push himself forward, and waited in the hall. He sounded delighted when Jolly said:

'Mr. Rollison is in, sir, and will see you.'

'Why, that's fine,' said Merino. 'Fine!'

Jolly took his hat and led the way to the door.

Rollison, who loved the bizarre, moved swiftly, lifted the hangman's rope from the wall behind him and put it on the desk; the loop was near one end, and it looked exactly what it was. Then he stood up, smiling. Merino made no attempt to shake hands, but his white teeth gleamed vividly against his black beard and moustache. Rollison was impressed by his size, his animal grace of movement, and by the gleam in his large, wide-set grey eyes.

'So you're Mr. Rollison,' he said. 'I'm very glad to meet you, sir.' He pronounced 'very' as 'vurry', and Rollison guessed that he came from the Southern States.

'And you're Mr. Merino,' murmured Rollison. 'Won't you sit down?'

Merino's smile broadened as he sat down and stretched out his legs. He didn't speak until he had assessed every feature of Rollison's face, and appeared uninterested in the fact that Rollison was studying him just as closely—even to the small mole on his right nostril and a small scar, about half an inch long, above his left eye.

'Cigarette,' asked Rollison, sitting down and pushing a silver box across the desk.

'No thanks—I only smoke cigars,' said Merino.

That was a lie; unless someone other than he had smoked

two of the cigarettes at the Lilley Mews·flat.

'I must say I'm very glad to know you,' Merino said, 'because I think you and I can do business together, Mr. Rollison. I think I ought to make a start by telling you that I'm a *very* bad man.'

Rollison's eyes twinkled.

'I can well believe it,' he said.

'And one of the reasons I want to see you is to find out what kind of man you are,' said Merino. 'You're quite smart in a kind of way, although I don't know that I like that particular way.'

'Well, you started it,' murmured Rollison.

'Meaning what?'

'Meaning Byngham Court Mansions,' said Rollison.

'I suppose you can look at it that way if you want to,' agreed Merino. 'Mr. Rollison, I'm not admitting anything. I'm not even accusing you of anything, although I will say that whoever came into my flat did a mighty good job. It's a pity I didn't leave the combination number in my desk. But that needn't come between us, Mr. Rollison. I've come to show you something.' He put his hand to his inside breast-pocket and brought out a black jewel-case. He put this on the desk and pushed it towards Rollison. It caught against the rope; not once had Merino appeared to notice the rope.

Rollison asked: 'What's that?

'It's just a sample from my safe,' said Merino. 'Go on, open it. It won't bite you.'

Rollison took a handkerchief from his pocket and held the case. He opened it by picking at the catch with his finger nail and, without once touching the case itself with his bare fingers, put it down, open, on the desk.

He did all this without a change of expression, a remarkable feat, because the sight in front of him was astonishing. There were three huge diamonds, stones which glittered and scintillated; beautiful things, worth a fortune.

'They would have been worth taking, wouldn't they?' Merino asked.

'Perhaps your visitor only wanted to see what was there,' murmured Rollison.

'Perhaps.' Merino spoke more quietly, and his voice wasn't so deep; it was the man who had telephoned the previous night and probably the man whose voice so frightened Barbara Allen.

'Maybe, too, he knows what he would have seen, now. There were several other cases; I just brought this along as a sample.'

'I'm not in the market,' murmured Rollison.

'Now that's just what I want to find out,' said Merino. 'Jewels fascinate me, I guess. And they're big money. I'm used to big money in everything I do, Mr. Rollison, I'm not a chiseller. Big money speaks. You're a good-looking man, aren't you? And I guess you've a girlfriend tucked away somewhere, a girlfriend who would like to wear diamonds like these.'

Rollison said: 'Ah.'

Merino had come to buy him off, and that in itself was a tribute. He showed no change of expression, but opened a drawer in his desk and took out a watchmaker's glass and a pair of tweezers. Then he pulled the table-lamp nearer to him —it was a modern office type, which bent in all directions— and switched it on, although it was broad daylight. He picked up one of the diamonds in the tweezers and stuck the glass in his left eye. He was conscious of Merino's steady gaze, but he did not hurry. He turned the diamond round and round, looking at the dazzling facets under the bright light, from all angles.

He put it down at last, let the glass drop and caught it.

'Sure, that stone's real,' said Merino. 'And it's not so expensive as you might think. Say, Mr. Rollison, do you know the Riviera at this time of the year?'

'Yes.'

'Well, prices are inflated, I guess, but you could have a good vacation on the Riviera for six or seven hundred pounds. That would last you three or four weeks, if you didn't have bad luck at the tables. That's what this diamond would cost you—just six or seven hundred pounds!'

'And a trip to the South of France?'

'Why, surely. That goes with it,' said Merino.

Rollison put the diamond back in the case.

'Why have you come here in person, Merino?' he asked.

'You don't need to ask that,' Merino said slowly. 'You've been to my flat, you know what I look like, you know Pauline —you've even met Blane twice. That means there isn't any way of hiding myself from you, Mr. Rollison, and I always prefer to come right out into the open if I can't stay out of sight. I haven't any quarrel with you, and I'd like you to have that vacation. Your man looks as if he could do with a holiday, too,' he added, and Rollison smiled faintly; no doubt that Jolly was listening at the door. 'You wouldn't take my advice last night, Mr. Rollison. Now you've another chance *and* you stand to gain something.'

'What will the Allens gain?' asked Rollison.

'They're outside this arrangement,' said Merino, with a slight hardening of his voice. 'I don't want to be misunderstood, Mr. Rollison, the Allens are no concern of yours. I'm no concern of yours. Blane—well, I shall have to restrain Blane, he would like to have a crack back at you, but I won't allow it—provided you take this vacation.'

Rollison leaned forward, placing his elbows just inside the noose of the rope.

'There are other kinds of holidays,' he said conversationally. 'Blane could tell you about that, I think. The kind I mean sometimes lasts for years. They cost nothing, except the loss of a little freedom.'

'That wouldn't suit me,' said Merino.

'I didn't think it would.' Rollison glanced at the telephone. 'My man doesn't look very tough but he's stronger than he looks,' he said. 'I can telephone Scotland Yard and have a detective here inside a quarer of an hour, and I can tell him just what you've offered, why you've come, what you've done to the Allens.'

'You could, but you won't,' said Merino.

'You sound very sure.'

'Of course I'm sure,' said Merino. 'Because you've been foolish in some ways, Mr. Rollison. I could produce evidence that you've broken into my flat. I could produce more evidence that you attacked Blane and nearly killed him. That's a criminal offence even in this country, I guess. And because you're known to Scotland Yard, well, I guess it would go even harder with you than it would if you were a stranger to them.'

'Evidence?' said Rollison.

'Oh, sure. Blane's. Pauline's. My own. You see, Mr. Rollison, anyone who works for me is prepared to swear anything I tell them to. And nothing is known against Blane or Pauline or me; we wouldn't be bad witnesses. And what could *you* do? Produce the Allens, maybe, to say they recognised Blane? No, sir, they wouldn't do that. Allen wouldn't dare, nor would his wife, even if Blane did cut some of her hair off. Maybe the police would believe your story, and maybe you've guessed the truth, or part of it, but—I know the law of this country, and I know what's *evidence.* Up to now, there isn't a thing that could be used against Pauline or me.'

'Possibly not,' drawled Rollison. 'That's what I want to put right.'

'But you can't put it right,' declared Merino. 'Because if you refuse to take that little holiday—well, I don't like resorting to threats, but you wouldn't be able to produce *any* kind of evidence, any place. A corpse can't talk.'

'Now you're talking a familiar language,' said Rollison.

'Maybe it's language you understand, but I don't particularly want to use it. You see, I don't believe in violence except in certain cases——'

'Such as Bob Allen,' interrupted Rollison.

'I'm not here to discuss Allen,' said Merino. 'Now, what about coming into the market for those diamonds? You can guess how much they're worth. Nearly a hundred thousand pounds, and that's a lot of money—you wouldn't have to pay tax on it either, Mr. Rollison. Your holiday wouldn't take much out of it, you can live in luxury for years. Now you've got to admit that's a mighty generous offer.'

'Yes,' said Rollison, 'but I can live in luxury without it.'

Merino sat back. His eyes were curiously light in colour and glinted with what might have been impatience or even the beginning of anger.

'That's where wou're wrong,' he said. 'You can't live at all if you don't accept, Mr. Rollison. Maybe you think I'm bluffing. Well, just put this question to yourself. 'I've come here to offer you those diamonds, which are worth a lot of money, and I wouldn't try to buy you off if the rest weren't worth a lot more. The stakes are very big. I can afford to make a gift like that and not notice it. But if you don't accept and you happened to find a way of getting me in bad with the police, I'd lose it all. I am not going to lose it all.'

'Aren't you?' asked Rollison, softly.

'No, sir! But I guess we're getting too serious,' declared Merino, flashing a smile. 'You're not going to be fool enough to refuse! Let's call it a deal, Mr. Rollison.'

'No deal,' said Rollison.

'Now, come!'

'No deal,' repeated Rollison firmly.

Merino sat for a long time, looking at him. The flat was silent; Merino didn't move and Rollison did not avoid his challenging gaze. It seemed as if Merino were trying to outstare him, to force him into submission by the sheer strength of his personality. And it wasn't easy to sit and watch him.

The silence dragged on, but Rollison was determined not to break it.

Merino did.

'You're a *very* obstinate man,' he declared, 'and I'm sorry about it, Mr. Rollison, but I couldn't talk straighter than I have done. I've given you warnings and I've made a very generous offer. What I can't give you is *time*. I'm in a hurry to concentrate on the main part of my business, and this isn't it. You'll go abroad. You won't see the Allens again. Or else——'

'You'll shoot me where I sit,' said Rollison dryly.

'Maybe I could do that,' said Merino, 'but first——'

The telephone bell rang.

Merino glanced at his watch, and it seemed to Rollison that he gave a sly grin of satisfaction. Rollison leaned forward and picked up the receiver. His voice was quite casual as he said:

'Rollison speaking.'

'Rollison, it's Allen here.' He recognised Allen's voice, even the note of desperation in it. 'Rollison, my wife—where's my wife?'

'I don't understand you,' said Rollison, very slowly.

'Don't talk like a fool! She was coming to see you, she ought to have been back an hour ago.'

'She hasn't been here.' Rollison looked at Merino, who smiled and stroked his beard. 'How long has she been gone?'

'Since two o'clock—just after your man called and told her to come. Rollison, if you——'

Merino leaned forward and deliberately put his finger on the receiver rest, cutting Allen off. Rollison kept the receiver in his hand; Merino kept his finger in position.

'You see, Rollison, I have several tricks,' he said, softly, 'Mrs. Allen was persuaded to come to see you, but of course she didn't arrive. She won't arrive, she won't return to her husband, she won't turn up again anywhere unless—well, you *might* find her on the Riviera. Are you beginning to understand what I say?'

CHAPTER TEN

BLUFF CALLS BLUFF

UNDOUBTEDLY Merino meant what he said. He sat back, completely at ease. Between his beard and moustache his lips showed very red. His eyes were creased at the corners, as if he were really amused and confident that he would get his way. It was obvious that he was used to being obeyed; probable that he would find it difficult to get used to defiance. His confidence was as remarkable as the fact that he was prepared to offer an enormous bribe in order to set both the law and police at naught.

He had expected that call from Allen; the timing had been perfect.

Now, his expression seemed to say: 'You haven't any choice.'

Rollison picked up the hangman's rope and drew it through his fingers, and for the first time Merino's eyes flickered towards it. His smile disappeared, and he sat more upright in his chair.

'Well, Mr. Rollison? What's your decision?'

'I think I'll tell you a story,' said Rollison mildly. 'There was once a very clever young man, an intellectual, a man who thought that he could defy Scotland Yard and all the police put together. And he did, for a long time. No one suspected him of crime, of murder—of a dozen-and-one offences against the law of the land and against ordinary human decency. I came to know him slightly. I had a great admiration for his cleverness, Merino—*he* wasn't a fool, either. And I think he might have got away with murder and most of his crimes but—he fell in love with a girl. A nice girl. Not his type, not in his set and married. He didn't worry about that. He always got what he wanted. He began to play on that girl's nerves. He did so by working on her husband and framing him for crimes he hadn't committed. He tormented and tortured both of them. He thought the time would come when he would get the girl, but—that was his mistake. This is the result.'

He lifted the rope.

Merino said: 'You can't frighten *me*.'

'Oh, I didn't frighten the man this rope hanged,' said Rollison, 'but he *was* hanged. I often wonder whether he would have been, had he let that girl alone. *I* didn't get him, nor did the police. We both helped, but the real thing that broke that man's neck was a thing he hadn't thought of. Love. Boy-loves-girl. Get a real case of that, and it's stronger than anything else. Barbara Allen and her husband are a curious parallel.'

'You may think that's so,' said Merino, but there was a slight huskiness in his voice which hadn't been there before. 'I can do what I like with the Allens.' He looked at the rope again, as Rollison kept drawing it between his fingers. 'And I've told you the truth, Rollison, but you've lied. That rope didn't hang anyone, it——'

'Oh, it's the same rope,' said Rollison. 'How I got it won't interest you, except—people said it was quite impossible to obtain!' He smiled. 'I've many friends, inside and outside Scotland Yard. You may think you know something about me, that I'm supposed to be a free-lance who sticks his nose into crime and works independently of the police, but—I've seldom worked alone, although I've sometimes worked without consulting the police.' He turned round suddenly and took a knife from the wall. It was of the stiletto type, with a handle of beautifully worked silver. He balanced it on his fingers as he went on:

'There's an instance. I took that out of a man's heart, Merino. The victim had tried to get away with murder and worse, and he was hunted by people he'd victimised—and I helped those people. Not with the intention of letting them kill him, I wanted to see him hanged, but events got ahead of me. I couldn't have helped by telling the police. I might have made the situation worse. There wasn't any evidence of murder against the man—so the police didn't come in until the body was found. I found it and sent for them; this was an exhibit at the inquest.' He tossed it up, and the blade glistened in the light.

'A nice clean job. I don't know where the killer is now, I couldn't even have produced evidence that he was the killer, but I knew it all right. Queer things happen in this hunt of criminals, Merino, things such as you've never heard about. They will again. And——' He stood up suddenly, and laughed. 'My dear chap, you're already half-crazy! You can't *buy* licence to put men and women into hell. I've no evidence against you now, it wouldn't help if I were to send for the police, although if it would, I'd tell 'em and let the Allens work out their own salvation. But—if anything happened to me, the police would know everything. And my friends wouldn't hesitate to take revenge.'

'You've got a clever tongue, but it won't help you,' said Merino, after a pause. He stood up slowly. 'I'm giving you another chance to take that vacation.'

Their eyes burned at each other. Merino leaned forward, put the jewels back into the case, closed it and slid it into his pocket.

'Don't blame me,' he said.

'I won't blame anyone,' said Rollison. 'No, don't go for a moment.' He pressed a bell at the side of his desk.

Merino stared——

Jolly did not come immediately.

Rollison's heart began to beat in a queer, spasmodic fashion. From the first he had seen the possibility that this man had brought others; that while they had been talking, Jolly had been attacked and overpowered. Merino might have more to his bluff than had appeared.

And then the door opened.

'You rang, sir?' said Jolly.

'I rang,' said Rollison. 'Bring in your camera, Jolly, will you?'

'Yes, sir.' Jolly went out—but before he closed the door he mouthed a word, a short word, which Rollison did not understand. It might mean a warning—that Jolly had seen someone else outside. Rollison turned that over in his mind as Merino backed slowly towards the door.

He said harshly:

'What's this about a camera?'

'You're going to have your photograph taken,' said Rollison.

'To hell with that! I——'

'You're going to have your photograph taken,' Rollison insisted. He opened a drawer in his desk and took out an automatic. He glanced down at it, opened the magazine, and held it so that Merino could see inside. 'Loaded, and don't say I daren't use it. Merino, if you were to get hurt through resisting, Jolly and I would concoct a story. That you came with menaces and tried to do me violence and got hurt in the process. That would be real evidence, as we'd both be eye-witnesses.' He laughed at Merino's savage expression.

'Not all the bluffs on one side. Ah—Jolly!'

Jolly mouthed that word again but still Rollison did not get

71

it. He put it to the back of his mind as Jolly came forward with his camera and equipment. The latter had only recently taken up this hobby seriously, although he had always done some photography for The Toff. He had perfected his camera-work—the flash-light and bowl were there—and he held it high.

Merino bellowed: 'Put that down!'

He made a rush for Jolly, who skipped nimbly to one side.

Rollison rounded the desk, Merino glanced at him, as if afraid that he would shoot, but when Rollison missed a chance, Merino shouted again and struck out at the camera and the bulb. He missed. Rollison reached him, poked the gun in his ribs and caught his right arm in a half-Nelson. Merino gasped with the sudden pain.

The light flashed!

Rollison released the big man and stepped aside.

'Would you like one without the beard, sir?' asked Jolly politely.

'Without——' roared Merino.

'Not a bad idea,' said Rollison. Merino swung round on him, but this time the gun was pointed towards his chest. Rollison's expression had altered completely; he looked grim and dangerous.

Rollison said: 'See if it's real. The beard, not Merino.'

'Very good, sir.' Jolly stepped forward swiftly and, before Merino could jerk his head away, took a hearty tug at the beard. Merino gasped. Jolly darted back, saying as he did so:

'It appears to be real, sir.'

'We could shave it off,' mused Rollison.

Merino backed towards the wall. His red lips were parted and drawn back from his white teeth. He was rigid with rage and Rollison believed that whatever the danger, Merino would try to do violence if they approached him.

'But, sir,' went on Jolly, 'I believe the police are able to remove the beard in a photograph sir, and by a process of facial measurement, identify the man, even though, when apprehended, he has no beard. Of course if you would prefer me to get the razor——' He broke off, inquiringly.

'Next time,' decided Rollison.

'There won't be any next time,' breathed Merino, and all his swaggering bravado had gone. 'I'll have the pair of you fixed, I'll——'

'Now don't make me change my mind,' advised Rollison. 'Jolly's a very good barber.'

'You've had your chance, you'll regret you've done this to me!'

'Oh, vanity, where is your common sense?' sighed Rollison. 'There's always an advantage in playing against a man as swollen in conceit as you are, Merino. Get out.'

Merino moistened his lips, then turned his back and went into the hall. Jolly went across the room, passed the man and opened the front door. Merino did not look at him, but as he stepped over the threshold, Rollison called:

'Merino.'

The big man stopped and looked round.

'Don't try any more rough stuff on the Allens. And see that Mrs. Allen returns to her flat to-day. Otherwise——'

Merino shot him a furious look, and went out of the flat. Jolly quietly closed the door.

Rollison looked out of the window and saw Merino get into the cream Chrysler. He was alone, and no one else was in sight. The Chrysler its engine making hardly any noise, disappeared round the corner.

'I did wonder whether we should follow him,' Jolly remarked.

'Let him sweat,' said Rollison. 'Nicely done, Jolly. But now, confess and admit that you got quite a kick out of it—much more than if he'd been photographed at Scotland Yard.'

'I did feel a slight exhilaration, sir,' conceded Jolly. 'I was particularly glad that we thought of taking his photograph. Also he showed that he was opposed to having it taken, which suggests that he is now somewhat worried about the possible consequences. The quicker we get some prints of that picture the better, sir.'

'While we're about it, we'll get a picture of Pauline Dexter. That'll do Snub good, if nothing else.'

'Talking of M. Higginbottom, sir, he has returned,' said Jolly. 'I tried to convey that information to you. I am glad to say he came up the fire-escape. He said that he imagined it would be better to keep out of sight if anything were—er—on the go, as he put it. He is having a snack in the kitchen. I persuaded him not to show himself to our visitor.'

'Happy thought,' said Rollison, and glanced at his watch. 'By jingo, it's five to five! *Snub!*'

As he finished calling, the kitchen door opened and Higginbottom appeared, hastily swallowing a mouthful of 'snack'.

He was a young man of medium height, well-built and lean, dressed in neatly pressed flannels and a brown sports-coat. His curly, light brown hair was untidy and his face split in a broad smile. His button of a nose could hardly have been snubbier, and his merry blue eyes surveyed Rollison as he said:

'How I kept out of sight I just don't know.'

'It's much better that you aren't known to these people yet. Learn the story off by heart, with all the characters concerned, and then go out and hire yourself an opulent car. Try *Gordon's Garage.*'

'So I'm for the road,' said Snub.

'You may be. Take it to Lilley Mews, near New Bond Street, and put it into the lock-up garage number 5.' Rollison tossed him a key. 'Clean the window which looks out on to 7, Lilley Mews, where Merino and his lady-friend live. Have some trouble with the car and behave like an amateur mechanic— and make a careful note of all the visitors to number 7. It's a two-in-one flat so we're interested in everyone who goes in or out. Take the Leica, photographs might be useful. All clear?'

'Aye, aye, sir!' Snub grinned, and then looked troubled. 'The Allens?'

'I think they'll pull through,' said Rollison. 'I must fly.' He hurried into the hall and, taking his hat off a peg, said over his shoulder: 'I hope you had a good holiday?'

'All the sweeter for being the shorter,' said Snub. 'You forgot to tell me whether to carry a gun.'

'You can wield a useful spanner if it comes to the point. If Mr. Wardle rings, Jolly, tell him I'll be along in ten minutes.'

'Very good, sir.'

And Rollison went out, jamming on his hat and hurrying to the top of the stairs.

He tripped on a piece of string, fastened across them. He grabbed at the bannisters, saved himself from falling—and saw a small packet lying two or three stairs down. In a vivid moment he realized the possible danger—and he leapt over the packet, stumbled, reached the lower landing—and then a vivid flash and the roar of an explosion almost blinded and deafened him, and the blast pitched him forward on to his face.

CHAPTER ELEVEN

BUSINESS AT THE B.B.C.

THROUGH the pall of smoke which floated about the staircase and the landing, Rollison saw first Jolly, then Snub. He waved to reassure them. His head was ringing; and a splinter of wood from the banisters had made a nasty gash in his hand, which was bleeding freely. That was not the worst. Doors opened downstairs, and the occupants of the other flats hurried towards the scene, a woman calling out in alarm.

Rollison made himself stand quite still, and called:

'An accident. It's all right, just an accident.'

'*Accident!*' gasped a man who came out of the flat nearest to Rollison. 'The whole place was shaken!'

'Sorry,' said Rollison. 'My man was making an experiment. Jolly! Clear up the mess, and don't forget that message for Mr. Wardle.'

'*Very* good, sir,' said Jolly.

Rollison turned and went on downstairs, holding on to the banisters. He ignored the indignant coments of the neighbours, and smiled at them placatingly. When he reached the foot of the stairs, a motherly little woman holding a Pekinese in her arms—which looked up at him with protuberant eyes —cried out:

'Mr. Rollison, your face! And your hand! You must have them attended to!'

'I will, very soon,' said Rollison. 'Must hurry now.' He gave her a flashing smile, not realising that smoke had blackened his face and that there were several scratches from which blood oozed. Because of the black, his eyes looked feverish and his lips moist and red. He reached the street, took in several gulps of clean air and felt a little better.

Jolly appeared by his side.

'You should really come and have that hand dressed, sir,' he said.

'I will,' said Rollison. 'Shortly. You deal with these people, and when the police arrive, tell 'em I tripped over a string that was tied across the stairs, and the explosion came from a brown-paper packet. Don't let that reach the crowd,' he added in a whisper, as several people drew near. 'I'll be all right,' he added, although he felt as if he had received a heavy blow on the head.

'*Very* well, sir,' said Jolly.

'And tell Snub to keep out of sight,' ordered Rollison.

He turned towards Piccadilly, pushing his way through a thickening crowd, and saw a taxi drawn up at the side of the road.

Perky Lowe began to get down from his seat.

'Stay there,' Rollison said, and pulled open the door and climbed in. He sank back in a corner and Perky drove off rapidly. As they turned the corner, he glanced through the partition opening, and asked:

' 'Orspital?'

Rollison gave a weak chuckle.

'Not yet. Aeolian Hall.'

'Oke,' said Perky, 'but you need——'

'I'll get all I need there,' said Rollison.

'Well, you're the boss,' said Perky.

Rollison leaned forward to look into the glass of an advertisement mirror which was fitted in front of him, and understood why the little woman had been so alarmed. He smoothed down his hair which was standing on end, and brushed the dust off his clothes, then dabbed at the blood on the back of his hand. He leaned back with his eyes closed, still unable to concentrate, but by the time the taxi reached the Hall, he was pondering over the daring of Mr. Merino.

Had Merino himself fixed that string and set the trap? Had he had time?

' 'Ere we are,' said Perky. 'Want me to wait?'

'Please.'

'Okay—give you me report later,' said Perky. 'Not that it's much, Mr. Ar.' He jumped down from his seat and helped Rollison out—and Rollison certainly looked as if he needed helping. 'Sure you can walk?'

'I'm all right,' said Rollison, stubbornly.

He went into the large, rather gloomy entrance hall of the building. It widened a little further along, where a broad staircase covered with blue carpet led upwards. Rollison had an impression of blue carpet, dark brown polished wood and glass all about him.

Standing near one wall was a tall, well-dressed man in striped trousers, a black coat and a Homburg hat—Freddie Wardle.

76

Opposite Wardle sat a commissionaire in a uniform which had been copied from the police. The commissionaire stared in amazement and Wardle stepped forward gaping.

'Rolly!'

'Slight mishap,' said Rollison. 'There's a first-aid room here, isn't there?'

'Yes, of course,' said Wardle. 'Come along.'

He did not ask questions, but led Rollison to a wide staircase —not the one he had noticed. There were only a few steps, and Wardle led the way along a narrow passage with cream walls. He turned into a room which was painted white, there were rows of bottles and first-aid equipment, a hand-basin and some cases of surgical instruments.

'Better wash first,' said Wardle. 'I'll be back in a moment.'

He was away for several minutes and when he returned, Rollison was drying himself on a bloodstained towel. The colour had returned to his cheeks and he looked much more himself. None of the scratches on his face was serious. His hand wound *was* rather ugly, and he allowed Wardle to bathe and then bandage it. Throughout the operation Wardle made no comment—a remarkable reticence, which Rollison appreciated. At last the job was finished, and Rollison combed his hair and shrugged his coat into position.

'Much better,' he said. 'Thanks.'

'What the devil *are* you up to?' demanded Wardle. 'I hope you're not going to try any of your fancy tricks here, Rolly.'

'Not my tricks, the enemy's,' said Rollison. 'I don't know what they're going to do, old chap. Sorry. And I don't see why there should be trouble here; this happened before I left the flat.'

'Then why didn't you have your hand seen to?'

'I can't keep important B.B.C. personages hanging about like that, it's not good for morals. The *In Town To-Night* people are still here, I hope?' he added anxiously.

'Yes—I just popped along to make sure. Not all of them, but the two who're arranging Saturday's show have stayed on.' Wardle stood firmly in front of Rollison, legs slightly parted, arms stiff by his sides, 'Before you see them I want to know more about this business—why you're so interested.'

'It's quite simple,' said Rollison. 'A young fellow who's due to broadcast on Saturday—name of Allen—is having a spot of bother. I'm lending a hand. This is just a routine check, as

77

the police would say.'

'Do they know anything about it?'

'They will soon,' said Rollison. 'This can't be kept from them any longer. You'd rather have me poking about than the police, wouldn't you?'

'Oh, come on,' said Wardle.

He led the way out of the room and along the passage between the cream-coloured walls. Rollison looked about him with some interest, although he could not keep his thoughts wholly from Merino and the explosion. He noticed that the walls were partitions, and did not stretch as far as the ceiling. Names were painted on the doors. This was a large hall, which had been partitioned off into offices.

They stopped outside a door on which were the names: *M. T. Hedley*: *Miss Rosa Myall* and, beneath it in smaller print the words: *In Town To-Night*.

Wardle and Rollison went in.

A tall, youngish man in brown, and a short, attractive woman wearing a white blouse and dark skirt stood up from the same desk—they had been sitting opposite each other. Although Rollison was fairly presentable, his appearance was enough to justify their startled glances.

Wardle was more than equal to the occasion.

'This is Mr. Rollison—he's had a slight accident that delayed him,' he said. 'Miss Myall—Mr. Hedley.' He pulled up chairs, and they all sat down, the couple murmuring suitable condolences. Hedley produced cigarettes and Rollison lit up appreciatively.

'Well, now——' began Wardle.

'Wouldn't Mr. Rollison like a cup of tea?' asked Miss Myall. 'I can easily get one from the canteen. Or perhaps something stronger?'

'That's a good idea,' approved Wardle. 'A drink Rolly?'

'Tea, please,' said Rollison.

Miss Myall hurried out, but was back almost before they could start talking; someone else would bring in the tea. Obviously she did not intend to miss anything of this interview. Hedley fiddled with a pencil and looked thoughtfully at Rollison.

'Mr. Rollison is interested, as I've told you, in finding out the procedure by which you get the celebrities for the show,' Wardle said. 'You're particularly interested in next Saturday's

78

performance, aren't you—the day after to-morrow?'

'Well, just to take it as an example,' said Rollison. 'This is just Mr. Prodnose at work.'

Clearly none of them believed him.

'It's quite simple——' Hedley began.

'Every week——' started Miss Myall, and they broke off.

'Go on,' said Miss Myall.

'Go on,' said Hedley.

'Miss Myall,' said Wardle, in the tone of a man who was tired of shilly-shallying.

'Mr. Hedley's right, it *is* simple,' said Miss Myall. 'The chief difficulty is one of selection. There are so many people we *could* put on. They fall into three categories, I suppose. The celebrities who really *are* famous, who come along for a special occasion, such as the launching of a new film, or from a play that's been running almost for ever. Secondly, the sensational people——'

'Such as?' asked Rollison.

'Now what have we got this week?' asked Hedley. He glanced down a typewritten list. 'Well, like Allen, for instance —chap who was lost in Burma for several years, lived with natives all the time and only turned up again a few weeks ago.'

'Of course, he's exceptional,' said Miss Myall. 'We tried to get him when he first arrived but couldn't find his address, and we were pretty crowded that week, anyhow. Then there's the third category—not really exceptional but giving us a new slant. I mean, we might put on a miner some week when the coal output has been very good, or an engine-driver on a holiday week-end—or a man who runs *The Skylark* at some seaside place, or a passenger on a train which nearly had an accident. Or a busker—you know——'

'Itinerant entertainer,' said Rollison gravely. His head still ached, but he was pre-occupied by this information and by what he had already been told about Allen.

'How do you get hold of such people?' he asked.

Hedley shrugged his shoulders.

'Somebody always knows somebody,' he said vaguely. 'One of us might hear of an unusual turn, or a friend might mention one. Of course, P.R.O.'s and publicity agents help—although they put one across us now and again!'

Judging from his expression, Wardle disapproved of that comment.

'Take next Saturday,' Miss Myall said, referring to her copy of the list. 'We'll start with a wandering artist—a man who paints country-inn signs. Then we go on to a young Danish couple who are in England on a holiday—one of these hospitality-in-return-for-hospitality stunts; we'll probably put on the two people who've been staying in Denmark as guests of the Dane's parents. Then we've Billy and Jill Lundy, who are in a new film—comics,' she added with a sniff. 'Then there's Toni, the Italian tenor——'

'We'll never get him to stand far enough away from the mike, he'll blast our heads off.' Hedley complained.

'That can be controlled,' Wardle put in quickly.

'Trouble is, Toni will blast off before Dick can twiddle the control,' said Hedley. 'That's the lot, except for the man we've mentioned—young Allen.'

'And how did you get them all?' asked Rollison.

'Miss Myall was staying in a Hampshire pub last week and the wandering artist was doing the sign, so she roped him in,' said Hedley. 'The Lundys are a promising couple and we like a bit of light relief—some of the turns get a bit heavy, the mike scares 'em, you see. Toni happens to arrive in London this week, and a singing turn always goes down well, so we got in touch with his manager. The Danes are a follow-up, we've done something like this once or twice each holiday season. Allen—how *did* we get on to Allen, after all?' He looked at Miss Myall.

'Pauline Dexter,' said Miss Myall promptly.

Rollison looked blank.

'A regular *artiste*,' said Wardle. 'You ought to listen to your radio occasionally, Rolly.'

'I'm all for low comedy and *Appointment With Fear*.'

'I wouldn't say that Pauline Dexter's a regular *artiste*,' said Miss Myall, judicially. 'She has broadcast in several of the regular programmes, but isn't a first-rate broadcaster. She's being groomed for the films, I believe.'

'Ought to do well,' remarked Hedley.

Miss Myall bent upon him a dark look.

'Possibly,' she said. 'She was in *Town* a few months ago and looks in every now and again. She came along last week to say that she could put us on to Allen. It's a bit old as news goes, but it's still got a lot of human interest. Life among the cannibals and all that.'

'The Burmese are not cannibals,' Wardle informed her.

'They aren't far short, from what I hear of some of the tribes,' retorted Miss Myall. 'You did Allen's stuff yesterday, didn't you, Mark?'

'Yes,' said Hedley. 'Pretty good, strong stuff, too.'

'So you do a script beforehand,' said Rollison. 'How do you go about that with a man who hasn't broadcast before?'

'That's where the difficulty comes in,' said Hedley. 'We couldn't put them up to speak impromptu. It might be a Communist or a Fascist or anyone with a bee buzzing in his bonnet. We can fade 'em out pretty sharply, of course, but we don't want the programme to fall down. So they have a script. We have a man reading the script while it's being spoken into the mike, so that if there were any serious deviation, we could fade out. Not that we ever have to,' he added.

'But how do you prepare the script?' asked Rollison. 'Do you write it for them?'

'Now come, Rolly!' protested Wardle.

'Not exactly,' said Miss Myall. 'We have them here for a chat. They nearly always talk freely, because they love the idea of broadcasting—the few shy ones soon get used to it when Mark switches on his charm! And, generally, when the story is told we've enough copy for a twenty minute broadcast. That has to be condensed into three minutes. That's where we come in.'

'So you write the script from the story you've been told?'

'Not necessarily, and certainly not always,' said Hedley. 'Some people are professional writers—or stage or film stars— and know exactly what they want to say. They write their own script and we vet it. Sometimes the others make a pretty good job of preparing their own script, and provided they don't try to slip in any glaring publicity stuff and are prepared to keep it down in length, we don't interfere. Now supposing we were preparing a script for *you*,' he added casually, and without moving an eyelid. 'We'd lead in through the interviewer—Bill Wentworth, say, and Bill would start something like this: '*Probably no man in England knows as much about crime, except of course detectives, as the Hon. Richard Rollison, who's in the studio with us to-night!*'

'And then *you* would say,' said Miss Myall, who for some strange reason was writing shorthand notes, '*I have met a few bad men one way and another, mostly in the East End!*'

'And Bill would say, "*Mostly, or all?*"' said Hedley. 'And you would answer: "*Oh, there are just as many crooks in the West End as the East End, but I've met most of mine in the East*".'

'And something about liking East Enders,' chimed in Miss Myall.

'We'd bring in "The Toff" somewhere,' said Hedley obligingly.

'And mention Scotland Yard—or would you prefer to leave them out?' asked Miss Myall, looking at him keenly. 'I mean, Bill could ask you your opinion of the police, how you think the force could be improved, and——'

'I can see I shall have to have a stab at writing this epic myself,' said Rollison. 'It may be possible to improve the Yard, but I'm not up to it. I wonder——'

'*Will* you write a script?' demanded Miss Myall, eagerly.

'We'll gladly put you in on Saturday week,' said Hedley. 'We've never had a private detective before.'

'Or whatever you call yourself,' said Miss Myall.

'We can do with something a bit lively the week after this,' went on Hedley enthusiastically. 'It won't take much time, and you've a broadcasting voice—hasn't he, Mr. Wardle?'

'Possibly,' said Wardle dryly.

'Oh, if he talked as he's been talking now, it would come over as if he'd been broadcasting all his life,' declared Miss Myall. Hedley was equally eager; and for the first time Rollison realised that both of them really lived in their jobs. Next Saturday's was the 400th edition of *In Town To-night* and yet they brought to the 401st an enthusiasm as great as to a new venture.

'Do come!' urged Hedley.

'May I think it over?' asked Rollison, who hadn't the heart to say 'no' out of hand.

'Write your own script,' offered Miss Myall, grandly. 'We'll just vet it.'

'I *say*,' said Hedley, suddenly swayed by a new and brilliant notion, 'could you bring one of the crooks with you?'

'I think perhaps we had better stick to the point,' broke in Wardle, not reprovingly but because he had a rigid mind. 'Is there anything else you'd like to know, Rolly?'

Miss Myall and Hedley fell obediently silent.

Rollison said slowly: 'I don't know. I see how you get the

people, how you prepare the script—what time do they arrive here for the broadcast? Half-past five?'

'Great Scott, no!' exclaimed Hedley. 'People who haven't been on the air lose their voice the first time they sit in front of a mike, or else squeak or whisper. But as soon as they've tried it out once or twice, most of them are all right. So we have them here any time after 2.30, the earlier the better, for rehearsals. That has to be done, because they're all allowed a limited time. One man might take five minutes to read a script which another would read in three, or even less. Sometimes cuts have to be made or bits added on, you can't really tell until you've rehearsed. It's all right with stage and screen people, but put an ordinary man in front of a mike with a script perched up in front of him, and he dithers.'

'I can well believe it,' said Rollison. I suppose some *are* really shy. This man from Burma, for instance—does he really want to talk about it, or have you used a lot of persuasion?'

'He was all right,' said Hedley. 'Bit worked up. We did the script yesterday afternoon, and I think it will be good. You've got it, Rose, haven't you?'

'Yes,' said Miss Myall, and produced several sheets of foolscap.

'I suppose there isn't a spare,' inquired Rollison. 'If I'm to think about it, I'd like to——'

'Take one,' said Miss Myall, and thrust a copy of Allen's script into his hand.

'Thanks,' said Rollison. 'And thanks for everything else. Now, what about having a drink with me?'

No one said 'no'.

Perky Lowe took them to the *Chester Arms*, in a side street near Gresham Terrace, and they sipped their drinks—except Wardle, who took his whisky-and-soda in two gulps—and chatted, crossing the t's and dotting the i's of the discussion. Miss Myall was the first to leave. Hedley followed soon afterwards, and Wardle, who had a remarkable capacity for whisky-and-soda after office hours, gulped down half his fourth, lit a cigarette and eyed Rollison fixedly.

'What *is* all this about?' he demanded.

'I'll tell you later on,' promised Rollison. 'Very hush-hush, for the time being. Thanks, Freddie!'

They left the *Chester Arms* together. Perky came out of the public bar, wiping his mouth with the back of his hand, and took the wheel of the cab. Rollison went out of his way to drop Wardle at Charing Cross, and then was driven back to Gresham Terrace.

'Anything more to-night, Mr. Ar?' Perky Lowe asked.

'Anywhere special to go?' asked Rollison.

'No, Mr. Ar, I'm at your service, same as always. Shall I stick around?'

'I think you'd better,' said Rollison.

'Oke.' Perky pulled up outside the flat, jumped down and, as Rollison climbed to the pavement, held out a folded sheet of paper. 'My report,' he said proudly. That Chrysler made three calls—juicy bit, ain't she?'

'The Chrysler?' asked Rollison, blankly.

Perky threw back his head and bellowed with laughter.

'Cor, you are a one,' he gasped. 'The Chrysler cor! She's a beauty all right, though, wouldn't like to try followin' 'er in my cab on the open road.' He finished laughing, and then added hopefully: 'Let's know when it is, Mr. Ar, won't you?'

'When what is?' asked Rollison, taken unawares.

'Nark it! The broadcast. You're goin' to broadcast, ain't you?'

'There's been some talk about it,' said Rollison, chuckling. 'I'll certainly let you know if it comes off.'

He went upstairs slowly. There was a smell of burning—or of something which had been burnt recently. The lower flight of stairs and the landings had been cleaned up, but on the flight leading to his flat the damage was all too apparent. A small hole had been made in the wall. The banisters were gone, except two rails which stuck up like the stumps of trees—and the tops of them were blackened, they had caught fire. Part of the steps had been blown away, and a biggish area was badly scorched.

He opened the front door, noticing that there were several dents in it which had not been there before. The full force of the explosion and the debris had been blown over his head; nothing else could have saved him.

He stepped into the flat.

There was a light in the study but nowhere else in the flat, and he heard the murmur of voices. Jolly was in there and possibly Snub had decided not to go, in view of the explosion. He hoped Snub hadn't stayed here all the time—the movements of Merino and Pauline were well worth following.

He opened the study door.

Jolly turned round with a start of surprise, and from the depths of an easy chair Superintendent William Grice of Scotland Yard looked up with an accusing stare.

CHAPTER TWELVE

POLICE

GRICE was a brown-faced, brown-haired, brown-clad man; and perhaps the most formidable detective in the country. He and Rollison were old friends, but whether their friendship would weather this storm Rollison did not care to guess. He looked down at Grice with a faint smile. Grice's skin was smooth and his complexion almost perfect—only marred, in fact by a large scar on one side of his face and head. That was from an explosion in which he had suffered so badly that for several days his friends had despaired of his life—and it had happened in an affair in which Rollison had been playing a part. His high-bridged nose was white at the bridge, where the skin seemed to stretch across it. He had large brown eyes.

'Well, Mr. Rollison, he said heavily.

'So we're formal, are we?' asked Rollison. 'Get the Superintendent a drink, Jolly.'

'Mr. Grice has declined one, sir,' said Jolly.

'Then give him a lemonade,' said Rollison. He took the other easy chair, sat down and stretched his legs. 'Well, Bill? Detecting? Jolly, get me those oddments you were handling, will you?'

'Yes, sir.' Jolly went out, and Grice clasped his hands together in front of his chest and spoke without raising his voice.

'I always thought you were a bit mad, Rolly; now I know you are. Time and time again I've asked you not to try to tackle any kind of investigation when you know it's a police matter. Time and time again I've spoken for you, and you've been able to do a great deal more than any other private individual. You know very well that if the A.C. or the Home Office got nasty, you wouldn't be able to get anywhere near a job again. Yet you let a thing like this happen.'

'Bad man comes, tries to blow me to perdition—and that's

all the sympathy I get,' murmured Rollison.

'You won't get any sympathy. A thing like this didn't happen out of the blue, something led up to it. Here are some of the things. Several of Bill Ebbutt's toughest has-beens are holding a watching brief for you at a flat in St. John's Wood. A taxi-driver named Lowe, once one of Ebbutt's hopes, is driving you about. Jolly is nervous, and refuses to talk—which means that he's hiding something. Even if you don't mind having your own head blown off, think of Jolly sometimes.'

'As a matter of fact I've thought quite a lot about Jolly lately. He wanted to tell you about this before.'

'Oh, *Jolly's* got some sense,' said Grice. 'Well, what is it?'

'Mystery.'

'Now look here,' Grice began in exasperation, but Jolly came in carrying a large silver tray. On one end was a glass of lemonade for Grice was almost a teetotaller, at the other, a variety of 'oddments'. Jolly placed the tray on the desk and handed Grice the glass, then drew attention to the other things.

'The exhibits, sir,' he murmured.

There were photographs of finger-prints; the knife; all the oddments which had been taken out of Blane's pockets, each with a little tab attached and a description written thereon. There was a sheet of typewriting, and a swift glance showed Rollison that Jolly had noted down the times of the telephone calls and the incidents—and had them to the minute. All of these things were to be expected of Jolly, but the final thing startled even Rollison; for there was a cabinet-sized photograph of Oliver Merino on the tray.

'Well, well!' he exclaimed. 'Congratulations, Jolly!'

'Thank you, sir.'

'And what are these?' asked Rollison, touching some pieces of charred wood. There was also a length of string, burned at both ends, and a tin tack badly bent at the point.

'They came from the staircase after the explosion, sir. A policeman took some of the samples but left these, and I thought I was at liberty to remove them. I understand that the constable arrived while I was telephoning Mr. Grice. I thought it wise to inform the police, since it was so evident that violence was intended. I trust that meets with your approval, sir.'

'Warm approval,' said Rollison.

'I hope you've a good excuse for being so late, because when I make a report, there are going to be some nasty remarks.'

'Excuse?' Rollison frowned and looked at Grice as if perplexed. 'I suppose so—unless,' he added in a burst of inspiration, 'you were to go abroad until it was all over! The Riviera, for instance—I'm sure you'd love a trip to the Riviera. How much would it cost, Jolly?'

'Six or seven hundred pounds, according to one estimate I heard recently,' said Jolly solemnly, 'but I have no doubt that it could be done for considerably less. Is the lemonade to your liking, Mr. Grice?'

Grice, who was sipping, grunted.

'Can I get you anything, sir?' Jolly asked Rollison.

'No, thanks. Don't go through. I'm sure Mr. Grice will want to ask you a few questions.' He leaned forward and indicated the various exhibits with his forefinger, explaining what they were item by item, letting the story build up vividly. He kept nothing back, except his own visit to the flats in Lilley Mews. And he ended with an account of what had transpired at the Aeolian Hall.

Grice finished his lemonade.

'And what else?' he asked.

'Believe it or not, Bill, I think that Allen is in mortal terror of you and a police uniform, and I thought it worth while trying to help him without recourse to law. And if you'd like an opinion——'

'You know what I think of you,' said Grice heavily.

'This doesn't directly concern me. I don't think you will get anything on Mr. Merino or his girlfriend, I don't think you will persuade Allen to talk, I don't think you could hold anyone in this affair except Blane. There just isn't any evidence against Merino or Pauline, only a lot of suspicion. And I'm sorry you've come because now I suppose you'll have to take official action, and that may really blow the lid off. You might possibly drive these people underground, but even if you do they'll pop up again when you're busy on something else. And I'd much rather get it finished now; Barbara Allen can't stand much more of this pressure. Nor can Allen.' He leaned back, touching the back of his injured hand gingerly. 'If I were young and callow in the ways of the wicked, William, and if I didn't know that you're the most orthodox of policemen, I would now go down on my bended knees and ask you to do nothing until Saturday.'

'That's impossible!' exclaimed Grice.

'The poor, poor Allens,' sighed Rollison.

'Pauline suggested he should broadcast, therefore Merino wants him to broadcast, he was promised relief by Saturday —and now he won't get it. He'll live for weeks and maybe months on the edge of a volcano, wondering when it's going to erupt again, he'll lead his wife a dog's life—and all because Merino chose a noisy way of trying to do me in. Sad, isn't it!'

'You needn't expect me to take any notice of that kind of blather,' said Grice. 'Even if I would—and I certainly wouldn't —forget what you've told me, there's the report about the explosion. It'll have to be investigated. The story of Merino's visit here—is that Merino?' he added, looking at the photograph which Rollison had indicated casually.

'Yes.'

'Well, the story will have to be told and he'll be interviewed.'

'Oh no, he won't,' said Rollison.

'Of course he will!'

'Mr. Merino will have left his flat and will be at some place unknown by now,' said Rollison. 'He took his chance and lost it. I can't really understand the fellow. I could understand him coming and threatening, but it was crazy to do this—or allow it to be done—knowing that even if I were hurt, Jolly wouldn't be and the story would be told. But I'm pretty certain this will scare him out of town. You might get hold of his girl friend, but she wasn't here, there's nothing you can pin on to her. If you tackle the Allens, all you'll get is a re-hash of what I've told you. Allen's scared of the police, but that's not an indictable offence. You'll spend a lot of time and public money chasing round in circles, whereas if things were allowed to go on as they are, we might get results by Saturday night.'

Grice made no comment.

'Bill,' said Rollison thoughtfully.

'Yes?'

'If I were to pull a few strings and get the Assistant Commissioner's hearing, will you support do-nothing tactics—on the strict understanding that I take no serious action without telling you? You'll have to watch events, of course, you could put a man to watch the Allens and another to keep an eye on Blane and a third to watch Pauline. But once you come out into the open, we've had it. The Allens——'

'It's not like you to talk about pulling strings,' said Grice.

'This isn't an ordinary case. Two youngsters in hell,' Rollison said. 'If you doubt it——'

The front door bell rang.

'See who it is, Jolly, will you?' asked Rollison.

Jolly went out, and Grice and Rollison sat in silence, looking towards the door. Rollison heard Jolly walk across the hall,
but he was not thinking about the caller. He wondered if there
were the slightest chance that Grice would see the thing his
way. It wasn't really feasible. He was giving way to wishful
thinking, and——

He sat up abruptly, for a girl's voice sounded outside.

'*Is* Mr. Rollison in?'

It was Barbara Allen!

He had heard her voice often enough to recognise it, but
had only once heard anything like the same note of despair—
when she had uttered a single 'Oh', over the telephone.

Jolly said: 'Yes, madam, he's in.'

Rollison jumped to his feet.

'Bill, sit tight for a few minutes.' He reached the door and
called to Jolly, who was taking the girl to the dining-room.

She was very pale and her eyes were lack-lustre. She wore
a wide-brimmed hat which covered most of her hair. Her
clothes were crumpled and her shoes dusty, as if she had
walked a long way. The tone of her voice reflected her expression—one of dreary helplessness. She looked at Rollison
blankly. He took her arm and led her into the study.

'I've a friend with me,' he said. 'He knows all about it. Mr.
Grice—Mrs. Allen.'

Barbara nodded, but hardly glanced at Grice. She went to
Rollison's chair and sat down. With a weary gesture she took
off her hat. There was a red ridge where it had pressed against
her forehead. Some of the long hair fell out of place, and
revealed the short tuft. She leaned back and closed her eyes
wearily.

Grice had risen to his feet, and stood looking at her.

'What's the trouble, Mrs. Allen?' asked Rollison quietly.
'You needn't be afraid to speak freely.'

'Needn't be—*afraid*,' she said. Her lips twisted, and she gave
a bitter little laugh. 'I'm so frightened that I don't—I don't know
how to go on.' Then her voice quickened, she opened her eyes
and looked into Rollison's. 'Can't you do *anything*? Isn't there
anything *any*one can do? Must we go on like this?'

'We'll get over it,' Rollison temporised.

'Yes, but *when*?' A momentary fire died from her eyes. 'Oh, I know you're doing everything you can, but somehow I can't seem to fight any more. It's been such a long time, he's worse than ever—you've seen him, haven't you?' She hardly knew what she was saying, but Rollison was glad that Grice could see and hear her. 'I'd rather anything happen than go on like this. I'd rather be dead.'

It wasn't hysteria or anything approaching it; she was just despairing.

'You must tell me what has happened,' said Rollison. 'I know you left home, because you thought you had a message from me. What happened then?'

'I was stopped in the High Street, and two men made me get into a car,' said Barbara. 'I knew who they were and I dared not shout or attract any attention. I thought I might learn something and help Bob. They took me out into the country.'

'To a house?' Grice interpolated.

'No, A copse. Near Uxbridge. They just told me to keep quiet. They didn't do anything. It was—terrifying. The way they looked and talked. They talked about Bob. They didn't tell me what he'd done, they just said that if he didn't do what he was told to on Saturday, I wouldn't—know him—afterwards. And they didn't tell me what they wanted him to do, they said he'd know. They said they'd drive him mad if he refused, but—he *is* mad! He doesn't know what he's doing or saying. They've warped and twisted his mind and now——'

She broke off, covered her face with her hands and began to cry.

CHAPTER THIRTEEN

GRICE PROMISES

GRICE and Rollison took Barbara back to Byngham Court Mansions. As they left Grice's car, they saw a furtive figure slip into a nearby doorway, and Rollison recognised Dann, who was back on duty. No doubt Grice also knew that the East Ender was there, but he said nothing. He had been greatly affected by the incident at Rollison's flat. Barbara sat in the back of the car with her eyes closed.

She walked listlessly upstairs, and fumbled for her key in her bag. Rollison took it from her, and opened the door. The flat was in darkness.

'Isn't Mr. Allen in?' asked Grice.

'He—he ought to be,' Barbara said. 'But I never know what he's going to do. One day he'll go out and not come back, I know he will.'

Rollison switched on the hall light.

'I shouldn't worry,' he said, and when she protested against the platitude with a helpless gesture, went on: 'Until Saturday, there's a good chance that you'll be all right, and there's also a chance that it'll be all over.'

'I know they said so,' said Barbara, 'but I've kept hoping that——' She broke off, and pushed her fingers through her hair. 'I feel so ungrateful, she told him. 'Thank you—thank you so much for what you're doing. I know someone's watching the flat all the time, I'm not so frightened now.'

'You'll be looked after,' promised Rollison.

There was no point in staying, so they left her alone in the flat and walked downstairs. In the hall, Grice stopped and asked abruptly:

'Didn't I see one of Ebbutt's men along there?'

'Yes,' said Rollison.

'He might know something about Allen's movements,' said Grice. 'I'd like to see Allen—as a friend of yours, for a start, not as a policeman,' he added gruffly.

'Stay in the car and I'll find out what Dann knows,' promised Rollison.

He went along to the doorway where Ebbutt's man had taken cover. Dann came out of his hiding-place as Rollison called his name, but did not advance into the street.

'Grice is around, isn't he?' he demanded.

'He's turning his blind eye,' said Rollison. 'When did Allen leave—and how did Mrs. Allen get away, Bert?'

'Allen walked out on 'is own two legs, 'alf an 'our ago,' said Bert. 'Had a dame wiv' him. Some dame! Talk about a blonde, she was a blonde beauty all right!'

'Oh,' said Rollison slowly, for a picture of Pauline Dexter appeared in his mind's eye. 'Was Allen followed?'

'Sure—Sam went after 'em,' said Dann. 'Same as old Sniffer Lee went after Mrs. Allen s'arternoon. She was picked up by a coupla men who bundled 'er into a cab an' then neely ran

91

Sniffer down,' Dann went on. 'Sniffer told Bill—didn't yer know?'

'I knew something about it,' said Rollison. 'So they're getting rough, are they?'

'I'll give 'em rough,' growled Dann. 'Trouble was, Sniffer 'ad 'ad a couple.'

'Don't be hard on him,' said Rollison. 'All right, Bert. I should wait on the landing outside the flat until morning, but don't let Allen see you if he comes back. Telephone Jolly when he arrives, will you?'

'Okay,' said Bert, and withdrew into the shadows.

Rollison walked back to Grice's car and climbed in. Grice crashed his gears as he turned out of the carriage-way of Byngham Court Mansions, and was still in a silent, reflective mood. Rollison was not sorry. The stories which he had been told showed him with what care, cunning and ruthlessness Merino and his men were acting.

'Well?' asked Grice at last.

Rollison told him the East Ender's story.

Grice lapsed into further silence which was not broken until they were in Piccadilly. Then, squeezing between two buses, and with a taxi in front and another behind, he chose to re-open the conversation.

'I'll do what I can, Rolly. At least I agree with you that the girl will crack under the strain if it lasts any longer. I shouldn't do too much in the way of pulling strings, if I were you—it might upset the Old Man's apple-cart.'

'What can you do on your own?' asked Rollison.

Grice manoeuvred the car out of the traffic and speeded along Piccadilly—a sure indication of his frame of mind.

'Whatever official action we take, we'll have to move slowly,' he said. 'We'll put out a general call for Blane, but there's only your description to go on and, unless he's got a record, it won't be easy to get news of him. I wouldn't advise tackling Merino and this Dexter woman yet, in any case—I'd just watch them. I *shall* have them watched,' he added, 'but my men won't interfere unless their hands are forced. I'd like to see Allen— still as a friend of yours!—but if you can't make him talk, I'm pretty sure I can't. I'll put all this to the Old Man, and I think he'll see reason.'

'You're a friend, Bill! You'll let me know what he decides,' asked Rollison.

'Yes,' said Grice. 'Now go carefully, Rolly.'

'I will,' promised Rollison.

He watched Grice drive off, then hurried upstairs, and Jolly opened the door as he reached the landing.

'Here we are,' said Rollison, stepping in and tossing his hat to a peg. 'Grice is giving us breathing space,' he announced with satisfaction.

'I am not altogether surprised, sir,' said Jolly, 'especially after Mrs. Allen's visit.' He retrieved the hat and held it out to Rollison. 'Mr. Higginbottom telephoned ten minutes ago, sir.'

Rollison took the hat. 'Yes?'

'Apparently Allen and the woman Dexter have gone to Lilley Mews,' said Jolly. 'It occurs to me that you will want to go there at once, sir.'

It was dark in the mews. The only light came from the windows of Pauline Dexter's flat—and that from the side windows. Rollison, glad of the darkness, walked across the cobbles. The main garage was closed, all of the lock-up garages were also shut. He reached his own, and tapped—a short and a long tap —and waited for Snub to open the door.

There was no response.

He peered through the window, but it was too dark to see anything inside. He tapped again. The noise sounded loud in the mews. He stopped when he heard the plodding footsteps of a man, probably a policeman, in the near-by street. The footsteps passed, and Rollison, satisfied that Snub was no longer watching the flat from the lock-up garage, turned and looked at the lighted windows. Snub might have taken it upon himself to break in, and listen to what passed between Allen and the actress.

Then he heard a sound.

It was low-pitched, a gasp or moan—and it came from Number 5. He turned sharply and looked at the sliding door. It was open an inch—he hadn't noticed that before, but now he could see that it was not flush with the wall. He put his fingers into the little gap and pushed the door open further. Utter silence reigned—but was broken suddenly by another moan.

Rollison turned from the door and looked right and left— and then walked up and down the mews, making sure that no one lurked in the shadows. Satisfied, he hurried back to the lock-up, and widened the opening until there was room for him to get through. He stepped inside as another moan reached his ears. He took a pencil-torch from his pocket and flashed it on. The thin beam of light made eerie patterns on the shining body of the car—and then shone on Snub, who lay huddled up on the back seat! His hands and wrists were tied—that much Rollison saw in a quick glance—and something poked from his mouth; a handkerchief. In spite of that gag, Snub had managed to make some noise.

Rollison opened the door.

'All right, old chap,' he said. 'You needn't——'

Then he heard a rustle of movement behind him, and darted back, out of the car—but as he did so, something hit him on the back of his head. A second blow followed, much heavier than the first; he lost consciousness.

When he came round his head was aching badly, and he could not move his arms and legs freely. The pain ran from the back of his head, down his neck and across his back. He did not at first remember what had happened, but as memory crept back, he realised the truth. A man had been waiting in the garage, Snub had been allowed to make that noise, or else the assailant had made it, luring Rollison into the garage.

He kept his eyes closed, and tried not to think.

Minutes passed——

He thought at first that he was bound to a bed or a couch, then discovered that he could move his arms freely, he wasn't tied up. It was pitch-dark, and he wasn't sorry; any light would hurt his eyes. The blood drummed through his ears with the effort of movement, and he lay still again.

Everything was quiet.

Yet—he could hear *something*. Faint sounds—very soft music. It wasn't far away. He tried to move his head again, in spite of the pain which shot through it, but he could see nothing, and the drumming of the blood sent the other sound away. It might be his imagination. He relaxed again, and became aware of something he hadn't noticed at first—perfume.

Where was he?

The perfume gave him a clue—and now that he was more capable of thinking and reasoning, he realised that he was lying on a comfortable bed or couch. This might be Pauline Dexter's room. He couldn't remember the scent, but it was a woman's room, anyhow.

He had no idea how long he had been here, and could not guess how long it was since he had come round. Two things were important. He was alive and free to move. But he mustn't move too quickly. That bump over the head had been pretty hard, and——

What about Snub?

He felt sick with alarm as he thought of the youngster; then the alarm faded, for he remembered that Snub had been breathing. There was no reason to think that Snub would have been killed and he, Rollison, left alive. Odd how he took killing for granted in this business, although as yet—and as far as he knew—Merino had not ventured murder.

He heard a door open.

Something clicked, and a light appeared at the foot and sides of a door which was opposite the end of the bed. The glow was only a glimmer, but it enabled him to see the outline of the bed, his legs—they weren't tied—and a wardrobe near him. He turned his head. Near him, on a bedside table, was a lamp; he had only to stretch out his hand and switch it on.

Someone walked along the hall.

The footsteps faded.

A sound—it *was* music, perhaps from a radio set which was toned down—crept into the room. Then the footsteps returned, and he heard a woman humming in a lilting voice.

Then the door closed again, and the light disappeared.

Rollison put his hand to his side and groped for his cigarette-case. He found it, and drew it out. Then he groped for his lighter, and thumbed that clumsily. The light from the flame hurt his eyes. He lit the cigarette, then held the lighter further away, to get used to it. It needed filling, and the flame soon died down, He let the cap click back, and put both lighter and case into his pocket. The little red glow near the end of his nose was hardly a light at all, until he drew at it—and then all he could see was the tip of his nose.

He sat up.

Springs creaked faintly; it was a very comfortable bed. He hitched himself up to a sitting position. The blood drummed painfully through his ears and the back of his head seemed to lift from his neck, but he set his teeth and sat upright, and gradually the pain eased. Next time he moved, putting his left hand towards the table-lamp, there was less pain.

He found the switch and pressed it.

A subdued light filled the room.

He closed his eyes against the pain, but gradually opened them. He was able to recognise the room it *was* the flat in Lilley Mews, Pauline Dexter's bedroom. On the dressing-table was a photograph of the girl, and next to it, that of a film-star masquerading in the guise of a Greek god.

Rollison put his feet to the floor.

The pile of the carpet saved him from making any sound, but the bed creaked again. After a while, when he had pressed his feet firmly to the carpet, he stood up. He thought at first that he would faint with the sudden pain, but it cleared slowly and soon he stood upright. He knew that he would be practically useless in any emergency, with a head as bad as this. He stepped to the dressing-table with its long, frameless mirrors, and sat on the stool. There was nothing the matter with his face or forehead. He put up his right hand and touched the back of his head gingerly—and winced with pain. He manoeuvred the side mirrors, so that he could get a back-view of his head.

There was a large swelling, but as far as he could see the skin wasn't broken.

He finished the cigarette, feeling thirsty. He looked round the room, and saw a hand-basin in one corner. He reached it, half-filled a tooth-glass with water and, without troubling to rinse it out, gulped a little.

He finished the water greedily.

All the time he could hear that faint music.

He went to the door and tried the handle, quite expecting to find the door locked—but it was not. He pulled it open. Odd, that he should be quite free to move about as he pleased. There was no sense in it.

A light flashed on, so bright that he gasped aloud and whipped his hand to his eyes. He saw nothing for some time except a red light through his eyelids. He leaned against the wall, recanting his thoughts—they hadn't let him roam at will; this had been done so that he would think he could escape and then have his hopes dashed.

'Put that—light out,' he muttered at last, and opened his eyes a fraction, peered through a crack in his fingers.

'Oh, is it as bad as that?' asked Pauline Dexter, as if distressed. 'What a shame! But you'll soon be better. Come in and have a drink.'

CHAPTER FOURTEEN

'REQUEST'

SHE slipped her arm through his and led him into the drawing-room. In a corner a radio was playing soft orchestral music, the air which she had hummed a little while before. She helped him to sit on a settee and, when he grunted as his head touched the back, she made a moue of sympathy and, handling him gently, pushed a cushion behind him so that he could sit upright. Then she pulled a pouffe near, and lifted his legs on to it.

'You'll soon feel better,' she said. 'Whisky? Or perhaps you ought to have coffee, after that blow.'

She went to a table near the electric fire. On it was a round glass coffee-bowl, and the coffee seethed and bubbled over the heat of a tiny methylated spirit lamp. Two cups were by the coffee-bowl, and she poured out.

'Milk?' she asked, 'No, you ought to have it black, with plenty of sugar.'

She was dressed in a cream-coloured silk dressing-gown, fastened round the waist with a wide scarlet sash. On her feet were scarlet satin slippers. The frilly lace of her nightdress, or pyjamas, showed above the neck of the dressing-gown. Her hair was a mass of loose golden curls, her complexion pink as a child's; and she wore only a slight touch of lipstick.

She stirred the coffee and brought it to him.

'Thanks,' muttered Rollison.

After a few minutes his head grew easier and he was not so affected by the light. She pulled up a fireside chair and sat in front of him, leaning forward with her arms folded.

'You must feel terrible,' she remarked. 'Your eyes are all bloodshot, did you know? And they look glassy. But they haven't marked you, thank goodness—there are so few good-looking men about, that I hate to think of one of them having his looks spoiled.'

'Very considerate of you,' murmured Rollison.

She laughed, and her teeth glistened and he could see the tip of her tongue.

'So you can still find a retort,' she marvelled. 'I wish Merino hadn't taken the steps he has done—I'm quite serious,' she added, as if he had shown that he disbelieved her. 'I always think that persuasion is much better than violence, but he's so used to having his own way. The trouble is that this way has often worked for him in other countries. He's not English, you know—he's a Cuban.'

'Indeed,' said Rollison.

'Although I suppose one ought to call him a cosmopolitan,' said Pauline musingly.

'Committing crimes all over the world,' said Rollison.

'That depends on how you look at it,' the girl said. But now that you're here and we're alone, I've a favour to ask. I hope you'll grant it because if you do, you'll save yourself and the Allens and perhaps a lot of other people a great deal of inconvenience.'

'Merino's already asked me,' said Rollison, 'and I am not in the mood to go abroad.'

'Oh, I don't mean *that*,' said Pauline, her eyes wide and starry. 'I always thought that he was silly to try to bribe you, but he's been used to getting what he wants by offering money—or rather jewels—to V.I.P.s. He's been a jewel merchant for so long that he forgets there are other values. He hasn't really found his own level in England. I shouldn't be foolish enough to ask you to leave England. I won't even ask you to keep away from the Allens! Frankly I'm a little afraid that if Merino loses his temper he might *kill* Bob Allen, and I'm fond of the boy. Besides—the police would have to be consulted if murder were done, wouldn't they?'

'I think they'd appreciate it,' said Rollison.

She laughed again.

'You're rather sweet,' she remarked. 'Is that cushion comfortable? You wouldn't like another behind your head?' When he said 'no', she took a cigarette from a box near her, lit it, and then put it to his mouth—as he'd done to Allen. 'Now you look better,' she said, 'I like a man to smoke. Now, to my request! I want you to persuade Bob Allen to go through with the broadcast on Saturday, and to say *exactly* what I've told him to say. He can easily work it into his script, that can be arranged without the slightest trouble.'

'So he's objecting, is he?' remarked Rollison.

'He's so stubborn,' said Pauline. 'He flatly refuses to do what I ask, but I feel sure he will listen to you. He may not have shown you much respect so far, but he's impressed by you. If you exert yourself, you can arrange it.'

'So all I have to do is exert myself,' murmured Rollison.

'Yes—and not too much, I shouldn't think,' said Pauline. 'Of course, you won't *want* to do it, I know that, but I think you will. He's a nice lad, isn't he?'

'Allen? He——'

'Oh no. That boy who works for you,' said Pauline, looking at him with mock innocence; suddenly he wanted to wring her neck. 'The one with the funny little nose—I wanted to laugh when I first saw him, I should imagine he makes a lot of people feel like that. Isn't it odd,' she went on, taking a cigarette, 'that some people are born cheerful and everywhere they go they make friends and spread brightness and happiness, so to speak, and others—rather like your man Jolly—spread gloom. What *is* the boy's name?'

'Higginbottom,' answered Rollison.

'Oh *no*!'

'James Higginbottom,' said Rollison firmly.

'Oh, how priceless! Why, it would almost be a relief to him to die, wouldn't it, with a name like that?'

Then she lit her cigarette, and let smoke trickle from her lovely lips.

Her manner hadn't changed; she was almost frivolous, like a young girl let loose in adult society for the first time. And she was provocatively attractive, but for the first time since he had come round, Rollison felt real alarm.

'You do understand, don't you?' she cooed.

'Yes,' said Rollison. 'Fully.'

'And you *will* persuade Allen?'

Rollison said quietly: 'Yes, I will.'

Her eyes shone. She jumped up and clapped her hands.

'I knew you'd be sensible! I could tell it from the moment I first met you—Merino would have been much wiser to let me see you before he did, instead of playing that foolish trick with the nitro-glycerine. It was a risk anyhow, because there was no knowing who would be the one to stumble over it. It might have been Jolly, and although he wouldn't have been much loss to anyone, I expect you would have been angry—even angrier than you were. So that's settled.'

'That's settled,' said Rollison, heavily.

'I'm so glad!' He thought it wouldn't take much to make her pat him approvingly on the head. 'Of course, you'll have to play fair,' she went on. 'You see, a friend of mine will be

99

in the studio—it's so easy to get people into that particular studio—and he'll be listening. If Bob Allen should say the wrong thing, or anything foolish—well, then there would be an unexpected sound over the air. A shot. I wonder if a real murder has *ever* been broadcast?"

'And whom would your friend murder?' asked Rollison.

'Well, Allen perhaps—or you.' Pauline laughed. 'I know you could tell the police or warn the officials, and try to keep suspicious persons away on Saturday night, but that won't help you. You see, unless Bob broadcasts *exactly* as we want him to, you won't see that delicious Higginbottom again. It must be vexing for you to be trapped like this, but I think you'll be wise and not fight against it. A sensible man always knows when he's beaten.'

'Yes, doesn't he?' asked Rollison. 'Where *is* Merino?'

'He's gone into the country for a day or two, just in case there should be any trouble over the explosion,' said Pauline. 'You haven't told the police about that, have you?'

'No,' lied Rollison, without a qualm.

'I felt sure you wouldn't. You've something in common with Merino,' she went on musingly, 'you're so fond of your own way.'

'And where is Allen?' asked Rollison, interrupting.

'Oh, back at Byngham Court Mansions by now,' answered Pauline. 'He didn't stay long. I told him what was wanted and gave him a copy of the new script—it's not altered very much really—and told him he'd have to do it, or he'd know what to expect. I will say this for him, he's not a coward, we haven't been able to frighten him into submission. And I sent him away quickly because one of those pug-nosed men you've employed followed him, and I wanted to get the man away before you arrived. As soon as he'd gone, Higginbottom was dealt with. We're efficient aren't we?'

'No doubt about that,' said Rollison. 'Is there any more coffee?'

'Of course!' She took his cup, filled it and brought it back. 'I've given you a dash of milk this time, and not quite so much sugar. You're looking rather better. I suppose it's because you've a load off your mind now you've decided to take the sensible course.'

'Oh, do you?' said Rollison. 'Supposing I were to get up and tie you in a chair, telephone the police and tell them all about this—what would you do?'

'I'd keep saying "Higginbottom",' she declared and giggled. 'Or else "Snub". *Don't* be awkward, will you?'

'Are we alone here?' asked Rollison.

'Oh no,' she said, 'I didn't take a big risk like that—one can't always be sure that a gamble will come off—and you've such a reputation as a lady-killer!' She turned away swiftly and pressed a bell-push near the door. Almost at once there was a sharp tap. She called: 'Come in,' and a short, stockily-built man appeared, wearing a handkerchief over the lower half of his face. And just behind him stood a still shorter man, also wearing a handkerchief mask.

'All right,' she said. 'I just wanted to convince Mr. Rollison that I was telling the truth.'

The taller of the two promptly closed the door.

'And with a head like yours, you can't be feeling much like fighting, can you?' condoled Pauline. 'I wonder if you can drive yourself home?'

'I can get a taxi,' said Rollison.

'You may as well drive if you can, your car's in number 5,' said Pauline casually. 'We sent Hig—Snub off in the one he'd hired. He told us about that, he wasn't feeling very brave and I don't suppose he thought that would do any harm. Then we brought yours round here. Oh, you'll want the key of your garage.' She took a key from a pocket in her dressing-gown and handed it to him. 'We took it from Snub,' she told him. 'I like that year's M.G., don't you? The acceleration is good and the springing first-class. *Can* you get up?'

She stretched out a hand to help him.

'I can manage,' said Rollison.

He did not trust himself to say much. The girl's composure, the way in which she hammered every nail right home, was quite remarkably devilish. And yet, as she stood back and watched him with rounded eyes, she looked innocent, beautiful and delightful.

He stood upright; and his head did not ache so much.

'Why, you're almost yourself, you'll be able to drive without any trouble,' she said encouragingly. 'I'll get Max to take you over to the lock-up—unless there's anything else you'd like to say?'

'There's plenty I'd like to say, but it had better keep for another day.'

'Any day but Saturday.' Pauline went to the door and pressed the bell again. *'Don't* try any tricks, Mr. Rollison, will you? I really like your Higginbottom, and I could easily get fond of you. I don't think *very* much of the Allens, but that's beside the point.'

There was a tap on the door.

'Good-night,' said Pauline. 'Come in, Max.'

The smaller of the two men appeared; and Rollison had no doubt that it was the 'boy' who had been with the 'gasman' when this affair had first broken out into violence. Max showed a glimpse of an automatic, then put it into his pocket, holding it all the time. He opened the front door and a cool blast of air swept in.

Good-night!' called Pauline sweetly.

Rollison didn't answer.

Max led the way across the dark mews to number 5 and opened the door. He switched on a light which cast a glow enough for Rollison to see about the garage. He went between the wall and the car—it *was* Rollison's M.G.—and opened the driving door. Then, keeping his distance, and obviously prepared for Rollison to strike back, he watched while Rollison squeezed himself in and took the wheel. Rollison gave Max a sickly grin, pulled the starter and put the gear into reverse.

'Good-night!' called Pauline sweetly.

Rollison backed into the mews without mishap, although normally he would not have taken the wheel while feeling as he did now. He glanced round at Max, who stood by the open door, then drove off.

There was nothing unnusual about the streets of the West End. Occasionally a policeman plodded past, taxis and private cars moved about, there were a few pedestrians but not many in these side-streets. It was a bright night and cooler than it had been by day. Rollison found driving less nerve-wracking than he had expected; he could spare time to think. He wondered whether he had been right to come away—but he had been in no shape to plan and think, certainly not to take aggressive action.

He reached the garage at the back of Gresham Terrace, pulled up close to the closed doors, opened them and switched on the light; this was bright, and showed the neatly kept garage, two spare tyres, tins of oil and a few tools. He went back to the car and drove it in, pleased with himself because he judged it to a nicety, stopping an inch from the end wall, and then angry because he could dwell on such trivialities. He got out again, slammed the door and wished he hadn't because it sent a stab of pain through his head, and then turned to leave.

He stopped abruptly; there was something in the back of the car—something he hadn't seen before.

A hand lay on the back seat!

Someone was huddled on the floor of the car. Was it—was it Snub? Had that damned woman——

He peered inside.

He saw a pale face and a black beard and a small hole in the middle of the man's forehead.

This was Merino!

CHAPTER FIFTEEN

CORPSE

EVERYTHING changed . . .

Rollison stared down at the dead man, hardly realising then that he had driven through the streets with a corpse in the back of the car, without even a rug thrown over it. He saw, not Merino, but Grice. Murder—and one could not play with the police when murder had been committed.

Everything he had planned, the half-formed idea with which he had been toying, all faded.

He straightened up, unaware of pain.

The light shone on Merino's closed eyes.

Rollison moved slowly away from the car; he had not touched the corpse. The little bullet wound was a familiar enough sight to him; and the dark ridge round the edges, the trickle of blood; he had been presented with the corpse of the man whom he had thought responsible for all that was happening.

Grice's picture faded . . .

Pauline Dexter's replaced it, looking as she had when sitting in front of him, innocent-eyed, her brow puckered, her voice so light and silvery.

Rollison shivered.

Then, throwing off the tension which had fallen on him, he

103

went forward again, opened the rear door and stood looking at Merino, who was squashed into the back of the car, one hand lying on his stomach, the other on the seat. He stretched out his hand and touched Merino's; the flesh was warm, practically normal heat. The blood, glistening, looked as if it had just trickled out.

Merino had been dead half an hour, perhaps, possibly an hour, certainly no more.

Rollison closed the door.

It would be pointless to go through the man's pockets; anything which might help him or the police would have been removed. He did not doubt why this thing had been done; 'They' were determined to prove they were capable of murder, and it would make him understand Snub's danger still more clearly. Everything fell into place, except——

Had the girl done this?

Or Max?

Was the girl or Max the real ring-leader of this series of crimes?

Had they fallen out with Merino, because of what had happened that afternoon?

He went out of the garage and closed the doors, locked up and walked through the empty street with a chill wind blowing into his face. He walked slowly up the stairs at Gresham Terrace, and was relieved to see a light under the door. Only then did it occur to him to wonder what the time was; not very late, or there wouldn't have been so much traffic about. He fumbled for his keys, but before he could find them, the door opened.

'I'm glad to see you back, sir,' said Jolly quietly.

'Yes,' said Rollison. 'Thanks.'

When they were in the hall and Rollison was plainly visible, Jolly began to speak—then closed his mouth and hurried ahead, to open the study door.

'What can I get you, sir?' he asked.

'Aspirins,' said Rollison.

'Some coffee——'

'Just aspirins.' Rollison went to his arm-chair and sat down. Jolly returned with three aspirins and a glass of water. Rollison swallowed the tablets, sipped, said 'thanks' and then groped for his cigarette-case. Jolly took it from his hand and lit a cigarette for him.

'No one lets me light my own these days,' said Rollison.

'Indeed, sir?'

'But I'm not blaming you,' said Rollison. 'Jolly.'

'Sir?'

'I've just driven through the streets of London with the corpse of Merino in the back of the car.'

Jolly backed a pace, and looked appalled. But in a moment his mask fell back into place. It was some time before he spoke, and throughout the long silence he stared into Rollison's glassy, bloodshot eyes.

Then he said: 'Where is the corpse now, sir?'

'Still in the car—in the garage.'

'Isn't that a little unwise?' asked Jolly.

Rollison's lips puckered into a smile.

'Sometime or other Barbara Allen told me that I was like a breath of fresh air,' he remarked. 'You are obviously of the same breath, Jolly. Yes, it's damned silly, but it took me rather by surprise. You see, I didn't know it was there when I started out.'

'I *see*, sir,' said Jolly. 'You didn't, then, shoot Mr. Merino?'

'No, Jolly. I'm sorry.'

'I think perhaps it's as well, sir. I feel sure that had you done so, Mr. Grice would have felt that you were taking too much on yourself. The—er—body was planted on you, then.'

He broke off, and this time could not keep back his exclamation of surprise.

'But—but you didn't take the car, sir!'

'No Black Magic; it was borrowed for the occasion,' Rollison said. 'Jolly, we've much too much on our plate, and I've some really bad news. We could shed the body——'

'I was going to suggest, sir, that I should take the car and endeavour to do some such thing,' said Jolly. 'I feel sure that in the circumstances, it would be better if it were not generally known that we were concealing a corpse. I—did you say you had *worse* news, sir?' He looked appalled.

'They've taken Snub,' announced Rollison.

Only then did he realise fully the regard which Jolly had for Snub Higginbottom. Jolly's eyes half-closed, he raised his hands in a helpless gesture of dismay. Without asking if he might, he went to a chair and sat down heavily.

'Get yourself a drink,' said Rollison. 'I'll try one now, too.'

'Very good, sir.' Jolly went to the cabinet and poured out

whiskies-and-soda, one weak, one strong. The weak one he gave to Rollison. He sat down again at a word from Rollison, and sipped.

'You—you've no idea where Snub *is,* sir?'

'Not the foggiest,' Rollison told him. 'No easy way out of this, Jolly. I've been given an ultimatum, too. Er—what's the time?'

'A little after twelve-thirty,' said Jolly. 'I was getting worried, and would shortly have telephoned Ebbutt, in the hope that he knew something of your most recent movements. Snub— Snub *did* telephone though, it was his voice, I'm quite sure.'

'Oh yes. No blame on Snub or you. They let him send for me and then shanghaied him. And they weren't exactly gentle with me. A man named Max . . .'

Jolly listened to the ensuing recital without making any comment; and Rollison told it at some length, because that helped him to fix the details in his mind. He did not even hurry over the interview with Pauline Dexter, because he wanted to picture her, with that curious blend of naïveté and blaséness, wanted to remember the inflection of her voice when she had 'threatened'.

'And the question now is, what to do,' he said finally. 'I'm empty of ideas, Jolly.'

Jolly, looking a better colour, stood up.

'We *must* do something about that corpse,' he said worriedly. 'In most circumstances I would say that Mr. Grice should be consulted, but——'

'This being murder, he couldn't hold his hand,' said Rollison. 'He would immediately see Pauline and her staff, and might detain them. But Pauline was so very sure of herself. She must have other friends who are looking after Snub. She's relying on the danger to Snub forcing me to keep silent. And she isn't far wrong. There isn't much we can do, Jolly. Grice will have Lilley Mews watched by now; we can't take Bill's boys along and raid the place. Even *you'd* like to use them for this, wouldn't you?'

'I would, sir,' said Jolly. 'You—ah—might make a further attempt to persuade Mr. Allen to talk. If you know what is behind all this, you will have a much stronger hand.'

'Oh, I'll have another go at Allen,' said Rollison.

'On the other hand,' said Jolly, 'I really don't think you are well enough to see Mr. Allen to-night. I don't like advising it, but the best immediate course is for you to have some rest. Your head looks very nasty, sir.'

'Oh,' said Rollison.

'I hope you will agree,' said Jolly. 'Meanwhile, there is the question of the disposal of the body.'

'That must stay where it is,' decided Rollison, 'we can't cart a corpse about London. Jolly, bad head or no bad head, I must tackle Allen to-night. Get me a cab. And if this doesn't work, I'll get Ebbutt's boys to tackle Lilley Mews, police or no police. I mean it,' he added, getting up with an effort.

Jolly was about to protest but changed his mind.

Barbara Allen opened the front door of the Byngham Court Mansions flat so quickly after Rollison's ring that he knew she hadn't been asleep. In fact she was fully dressed although she looked tired out. A gleam of hope sprang to her eyes when she first saw him, but he shook his head.

'Nothing new, Mrs. Allen, but I want a word with your husband.'

'Oh, please don't wake him up,' she begged. 'He's dropped off to sleep, and——'

'I must have a word with him,' insisted Rollison. 'I wouldn't ask if it weren't essential.'

She gave in.

'I suppose you must if you must. He's in the spare room he went straight in there when he came in. He hardly said a word, and wouldn't have anything to eat.'

She led the way to a tiny room, where there was a single bed, a small table and a corner cupboard. Allen lay under the sheet, wearing his singlet and trunks. He breathed evenly, and when Rollison called his name, did not stir. Barbara looked tense when Rollison shook Allen's shoulder vigorously.

But Allen didn't wake.

Rollison pulled up his eyelids and examined his eyes; they were contracted to tiny pin-points, and he judged from them that Allen had been drugged with morphia. He felt his pulse; it was very sluggish. He did not think the youngster was in any danger, the dose was enough to make him unconscious, but was not fatal.

He told Barbara, and added:

'It's probably as well; at least he won't be worried for a few hours. Keep him warm—and then go to bed yourself. There's

107

absolutely no danger. If I had my way, I'd give you a shot,
that would send you off to sleep.'

'I haven't slept—not really *slept*—for days,' she told him.

One of the most expert cracksmen in the East End of
London had long since retired but, because of a service which
the Toff had rendered him some years ago, agreed to have
a look at the flat in Lilley Mews and to open the door. He
found little difficulty in climbing over the back of the garage
and dropping into Lilley Mews, without being seen by the two
police-constables who were unostentatiously hovering near the
entrance. What was more, he discovered an easy way over the
old buildings of the mews, and several of Bill Ebbutt's men
followed him.

The flat was entered.

No one was there; nor was there anyone in the upstairs flat.

It was after three o'clock when Rollison went to bed, and
after eleven when he woke up. His head still ached and was
tender where he touched it, but his eyes were clearer and he
could move about without difficulty or pain. So he bathed,
shaved and breakfasted, much as if it were a normal morning.

After telling him that Mrs. Allen had telephoned to say that
Allen had come round about nine o'clock, but was still in bed,
Jolly said little. The obvious thing to do was to tell Grice, but
every time Rollison thought of that, a picture of Snub hovered
in his mind's eye.

He had no clue as to where to find Pauline Dexter, no idea
where Blane, Max and the little man might be. Beyond inquiring at the *Meritor Motion Picture Company's* office, there
was little he could do to trace her. He telephoned a friend, who
immediately assumed that his interest in Pauline was amatory,
and promised to find out whether she had a cottage in the
country or a *pied à terre* anywhere else in London. He warned
him that Pauline was going about with a big South American.
Rollison promised to take heed of the warning, then rang off,
thinking about Merino. He had assumed that there would be
nothing in the dead man's pockets which might help, but it
was possible that some fragmentary clue would be found, so
he went to the garage.

In the street he was met by two men, one young and earnest,
the other middle-aged and genial. One represented the *Morning*

Cry, the other a Sunday newspaper. It was a quarter of an hour before they left him, apparently convinced that there was no 'copy' to be got out of him at the moment. Because of them, he went the long way round to the garage, and looked up and down the narrow road where it was situated, before unlocking the door. His heart began to thump; perhaps he was a fool to come here in broad daylight.

Even with the door open the garage was poorly lit by day, because of the backs of tall houses on the other side of the road, which hid the sun, and in any case Merino was dumped well down, out of casual sight.

He slipped inside.

'Going places, Mr. Rollison?' a man asked.

Rollison stiffened, but forced himself to turn round slowly and to look at the speaker, who stood outside the garage, showing a polite smile.

It was the middle-aged reporter of the *Morning Cry.*

CHAPTER SIXTEEN

TRICK TO JOLLY

ROLLISON turned his back on the car and leaned against it, maintaining his smile, and slipping his hand into his pocket for his cigarette-case. The reporter, named McMahon, was a friendly soul whom he knew well—but he was first and last a good reporter.

Rollison held out his case, standing so that McMahon could not get too near the car.

'Thanks,' said McMahon, who had no accent to justify his Irish name. 'Well, are you?'

'I'm always going places,' said Rollison. 'You take a lot of satisfying, don't you?'

'I was taught to believe only half what I see and nothing that I hear,' said McMahon. 'Come off it, and give me the story. And before you say there isn't one, listen to me,' he went on. 'Two or three of Bill Ebbutt's bruisers were out all night and I heard a whisper that they'd been on a job for you. There was that explosion on the staircase yesterday. Is somebody trying to get a flat by bumping you off?'

Rollison said: 'Well, you seem to know a lot.'

'Be yourself,' urged McMahon. 'You're not usually like this, you don't hold out on us.' He stretched out a hand and pressed it against the corner of the M.G., and if he came a yard nearer, he would be able to see Merino. 'Let's have it, Rolly. I'll keep it off the record, if you like.'

'Nice of you,' murmured Rollison. 'Perhaps you're right, Mac——'

'Now you're talking!'

'That's the trouble, I'm not at liberty to talk.' Rollison smoothed down his hair, wincing when he touched the bruise. 'I might drop you a hint, if that'll help.'

'Maybe it will,' said McMahon.

'There might be something interesting in Saturday's show of *In Town To-night,*' he began, cautiously, 'and——'

'Oh, come off it,' said McMahon. He took his hand from the car and came forward, and Rollison's heart beat faster, he found it almost impossible to keep quite steady. '*In Town To-night's* a nice gossip column, but——'

'Oh, this is special,' Rollison assured him. 'It might be sensational. Among others, the police will be present—although the B.B.C. may not know it. If you know anyone who can get you in——'

'I know Hedley,' said McMahon, and his eyes gleamed. 'Okay, Rolly I'll be there—I'll just breeze in.'

'For the love of Mike, keep it to yourself!'

'You bet I'll keep it to myself—one reporter's quite enough if anything's going to happen there! Got any background stuff, so that I can write it up beforehand? I'd like to catch the *Sunday Cry*—don't forget we've got a Sunday paper, will you?'

'I won't forget, but I can't give you any background,' said Rollison. 'Aren't you ever satisfied?'

'No, never,' said McMahon, 'but thanks. Nice car you've got here,' he added, and looked deliberately into the back through the rear window.

Rollison stood waiting for the outburst, screwed up to a pitch of icy tension.

'*Very* nice,' said McMahon. 'Which way are you going? If it's Fleet Street, you might give me a lift.'

Rollison gulped. 'I came to get some papers out of the car,' he said, and for the first time ventured to look into the back.

If Merino's body were invisible from the rear window, he might yet get away with it; it was quite possible that the corpse had sagged down during the night.

He couldn't see the body.

The body wasn't there.

Jolly looked up as Rollison entered the flat and remarked that he hadn't been gone long. Rollison gravely agreed and went into the study, calling: 'Jolly!' in a loud voice, as he reached his desk. When he turned round Jolly stood respectfully in the middle of the room, his brown, doleful eyes showing no expression.

'The body isn't there any more,' announced Rollison slowly.

'I'm afraid I must accept full responsibility for that, sir,' said Jolly. 'After you had dropped off to sleep, I couldn't rest for thinking about it, and I put the situation to Ebbutt, over the telephone. He immediately agreed to take the necessary steps. I understand that the corpse now reposes in a box in the cellar of a disused warehouse.'

'Oh,' said Rollison heavily. 'Trick to Jolly. You gave me the worst five minutes and the best split second I've had for a long time, and I freely forgive you.'

'Thank you, sir. And I have cleaned the back of the car and made sure that it can be used,' said Jolly, 'There is no fear of any fingerprints being found. Unfortunately there was nothing in Merino's pockets which would help us. But at least we have to-day in which to work without undue anxiety here. If only we had some indication of where Mr. Higginbottom might be, we could feel so much easier in our minds. I suppose you will find out what alteration was wanted in Mr. Allen's script as soon as you can, sir?'

'Yes,' said Rollison. 'I——'

The telephone bell rang.

He broke off and motioned to the instrument, and Jolly lifted the receiver, saying as if it were a refrain: 'This is the Hon. Richard Rollison's residence.' He had hardly finished before he lowered the receiver from his ear, and stared in astonishment at Rollison.

'It's her!' he exclaimed.

'Pauline!' cried Rollison.

He should have expected a call, should have known that her daring outclassed even Merino's. She would be as calm as she had been at the flat, and he must match it.

He took the receiver and said:

'Good-morning, Miss Dexter.'

'I'm so glad we're on friendly terms,' said Pauline, gaily. 'I heard you call my name out when Jolly told you I was on the line. How is your poor head this morning?'

'Rather battered,' confessed Rollison.

'I hope it's not so painful, you looked terrible last night,' said Pauline. 'I knew you'd feel like murder when you reached home, that's why I left the flat—and I shall stay away for a few days. I rang up to remind you that you must persuade Bob Allen to do what I've told him.'

'Not easily,' said Rollison. The way she had brought in the word 'murder' was clever—she used the same method of oblique approach as with her threats.

'That's good,' she said warmly. 'And *please* don't try to find me, you won't succeed, I've been so careful about everything. You found that package in your car, I expect?'

'Package?' echoed Rollison.

'Yes, in the back.'

'I found nothing worth looking at,' said Rollison. For the first time, his spirits rose. Pauline should have let well alone, and not given him a chance to confuse and puzzle her. This was the first mistake she had made, and had slipped into it so unwarily. 'There was certainly nothing in it this morning; the car's been thoroughly cleaned and the upholstery vacuumed. What was in the package?' Rollison sounded genuinely curious.

Pauline did not answer.

'You may as well tell me,' went on Rollison, earnestly. 'There isn't much you've kept back from me. By the way, how is Mr. Merino this morning?'

'What a beautiful liar you are,' said Pauline.

'My dear Miss Dexter,' Rollison said reproachfully, 'I don't understand you. I thought we'd sworn not to deceive each other. Let me go over the details again. I'm to persuade Allen to incorporate certain alterations in his B.B.C. script, so that your message can go out to your friends. That's it, isn't it?'

'I said nothing about a message.' Her voice was sharp.

'But you talk so obscurely that I have to read between the lines,' protested Rollison. 'And if the message doesn't go out as you've instructed, one of your thugs will be on duty in the studio to take aggressive action. *Very* thorough, Miss Dexter.

Shall I see you there?'

'You will not!'

'Oh, what a pity,' said Rollison. 'Because I think we ought to meet again before long—in fact before to-morrow night. I'm not at all sure that I'm doing the right thing by taking your instructions, but you may be able to convince me if we have a little chat. How about *Blott's,* at twelve-forty-five? I won't leave you in the lurch this time, and the waiter won't spill your soup.'

'Obviously you're feeling *very* much better,' said Pauline. I hope that doesn't mean that the police have been consulted. If they show up, you won't see Higginbottom again.'

He had so shaken her composure that she came out with a direct threat!

'No police—I always prefer working without them,' said Rollison firmly. 'If I were to tell them about you, my pet, I wouldn't be able to wring your neck myself. I'm looking forward to doing that later, but I'll do nothing violent at *Blott's.*'

Her voice lost all trace of its silvery note, became coarse, ugly.

'I've warned you what will happen if Allen doesn't alter that script.'

She was badly shaken, she had been living on her nerves, a tiny crack in her armour had quickly grown larger, perhaps large enough to destroy her defences.

'But he isn't even going to broadcast,' he said gently.

'*What!*'

'I've been thinking about it, and I've just decided that it will be much better for him to stay at home to-morrow night,' Rollison said. 'Pity in some ways; I think he would sound well over the air, don't you? But it just won't do, we can't use the B.B.C. for such dark deeds as yours. And you've slipped away into the country, after giving him a dose of morphia, so I'll give him another dose and take him away for a day or two. You've got Snub, I've got Bob Allen, and that about makes us equal. **Good-bye,** my pet!'

'Rollison!'

'What, are you still there?' asked Rollison, sweetly.

'Rollison, if you stop Allen from broadcasting, you——'

'Sorry, my love, but there's no drawing back. Good-bye!'

'Rollison!'

He rang off.

Jolly stared at him with glowing eyes.

'And that was a nice instalment of reward,' said Rollison. 'Jolly, telephone Ebbutt and tell him that I want to hide Allen away for a day or two. He must be able to collect him at short notice. I'll go and get Allen, and take him straight to the gymnasium. 'Right?'

'*Very* good, sir!'

Rollison hurried across the hall and downstairs, gladly enduring his aches and pains. The morning was much brighter, almost another day. He was angry with himself for not having thought of this before; it was so obviously the right thing, the only thing. Pauline desperately wanted Allen to broadcast. If anything could lure her out of hiding, making him vanish would do it.

He turned right, towards the garage, but before he had gone two steps a cheerful Cockney voice sounded.

'Want me s'morning?' demanded Perky Lowe.

Rollison swung round.

'You're just the man,' he said. 'Byngham Court Mansions, in a hurry!'

He was hardly inside the cab before it started off. He watched the passing traffic and the passing people with a benevolent eye, and now and again burst into a chuckle. He pondered over the new move, trying to see any way in which it would work to his disadvantage and perhaps put Snub in more danger; none presented itself. From the beginning, Merino and Pauline had been determined to make Allen do exactly what they wanted, and—he was necessary to their plot, necessary because of the proposed broadcast. Spiriting Allen away was the perfect answer to the threat to Snub.

A plain-clothes detective was in the street near Byngham Court Mansions, and undoubtedly he noticed who climbed out of the taxi which Perky pulled up close to the front door. Rollison hurried upstairs. When he reached the top, his head began to ache more painfully, but he was still in high feather. Sam was on the landing, and greeted him cheerfully.

Rollison rang the bell, and this time Barbara was no longer answering it. She looked surprised to see him, and her eyes were swollen, as if she had been crying.

'Well, how's the invalid?' asked Rollison cheerfully.

'He's—a bit better.'

'He's still here?'

'Yes—yes, of course,' said Barbara. 'He's getting up now.'

114

'And in a bad mood, is he?' asked Rollison gently. 'I shouldn't be too worried this morning. Tempers get frayed after you've been drugged.'

'He seems to have gone right back,' said Barbara. 'There are moments when I almost——'

She broke off abruptly.

Rollison said: 'What was this morning's trouble about? Any particular thing?'

'Well, yes—but that was the excuse, not the reason,' said Barbara. 'He's lost a piece of paper, on which there were some notes. I destroyed them by accident, and—oh, but it doesn't matter!'

She turned away.

'Don't let it get you down,' Rollison said quickly. 'I've an idea which will help, I think, and—we'll see it all through.'

Barbara didn't answer.

Rollison called out: 'Allen! Are you up?'

Allen called a surly answer from the big bedroom.

He was dressed, but hadn't shaved. He stood by the window, with smoke curling from a cigarette which drooped from the corner of his mouth. His eyes were lack-lustre, and he showed all the symptoms that might be expected in a man who had been given a dose of morphia.

'Now what do you want?' he demanded.

Rollison said: 'About this broadcast—Pauline Dexter wants you to make an alteration or two, doesn't she?'

'I don't see that it's any of your business,' growled Allen. 'In fact I've been doing a lot of thinking. Things aren't any better, they're worse than they were when you joined in. I was right when I told you to take your nose out of my affairs.'

'That's a bit hard,' said Rollison mildly.

'Maybe it is, but now you know,' Allen put a trembling hand to his lips, to take the cigarette out. 'I'm tired of it all!' he went on unsteadily. 'I've fought as much as I can, but I'm not going to fight any more. Pauline wants to have a say in the script—okay, she can have it. That's final. And when I've broadcast on Saturday night, it'll all be over—thank God, it will all be over!'

He turned away from Rollison.

Barbara in the doorway, looked from Rollison to her husband, but did not move.

Rollison looked at Allen's set profile and squared shoulders

—and the three of them stayed like that for a long time. All was quiet in the room. In the street, traffic passed noisily; a boy walked, whistling shrilly, along the pavement.

CHAPTER SEVENTEEN

PRISONER

IF Allen broadcast to Pauline's instructions, *would* Snub be all right?

And if the broadcast went off without a hitch and the woman's purpose was served, would it really help Allen or his wife?

As he looked at Allen, Rollison realised that the events of the past twelve hours had affected his own judgment. He had been seeing things too close up, had been too worried because of Snub, talk of the broadcast and the murder of Merino, to see the whole facts.

Something was to happen *after* the broadcast—a happening so important, worth so much money, that Merino had been prepared to give away those stupendous diamonds to make sure nothing prevented it.

The wearing of Allen's nerves; the lesser crimes; the capital crime; all these were due to one thing only—the unknown motive.

Supposing Snub were sent back after the broadcast, his life saved by giving Pauline the victory, would Snub rest happy? Would he, Richard Rollison, ever be conscience-free?

Rollison looked over the roof-tops, thinking on these things —and then glanced at Allen. And he saw in Allen's eyes a glint which hadn't been there before. It was a disturbing glimpse of something which he couldn't place properly, unless it were this: that Allen had been so whipped and beaten by events that he had become cunning and crafty in his all-consuming desire to let the woman have her way, and so be free from trouble.

What had happened between Allen and Pauline Dexter?

He felt, vaguely and yet with a stirring of a new alarm, that she had bent him completely to her will.

Allen looked away, and spoke roughly:

'Haven't you heard enough?'

'Yes, quite enough,' said Rollison. 'I still think you'd better come with me.'

'I'm staying here!'

Barbara broke her long silence.

'Won't it—won't it be better just to let Bob broadcast?' she asked. 'You said yourself that everything might be all right after Saturday. And if the broadcast can settle it, don't interfere. It can't do any *serious* harm.'

'I don't give a damn what harm it does,' said Allen harshly. 'I'll be able to rest, that's all that matters now. I can't stand this any longer, my nerves won't take it.' He shouted now. 'So clear out, Rollison!'

'I wish it were as easy as that, but there are complications,' said Rollison. 'Remember Snub Higginbottom?'

Barbara started. 'Is he back?'

'Where does he come in, except that he works for you?' asked Allen. 'I remember you, now. You were with him in Regent Street a few weeks ago—I told Barbara you looked as if you'd come right out of the pages of the *Tailor & Cutter.*' He gave a little, mirthless laugh. 'That isn't far out. Well, what about Snub?'

'He also lent a hand,' said Rollison. 'As a result, he disappeared. Pauline Dexter tells me that she knows where he is. I can't imagine he's having a very nice time, and I don't think they'll stick at murder if it serves their purpose.'

Barbara exclaimed: 'No!'

Allen swung round on her:

'You seem to have forgotten how to think or talk, all you do is to run round with a face as long as a wet week, bleating: "Oh, dear, what will happen next?" I'm fed up to the teeth with it.' He ignored the crushed look in Barbara's eyes, and turned on Rollison. 'Supposing Snub has caught a packet? That's up to him—and up to you. I told you to keep out of it. I couldn't have put it more clearly.' He stepped forward, and took Rollison by the shoulder. 'You know where the door is— you know it a damned sight too well. I'm wondering if this was your little love-nest while I was away. Bar seems to think you're the cat's whiskers.'

Barbara cried: 'Bob, oh, Bob!'

Allen pushed the unresisting Rollison again.

'Caught you out, have I? The guilty secret at last, and——'

117

Barbara said in a low, strangely clear voice:

'You've sunk about as low as men can sink. I've tried—how I've tried—to help you. But now——'

Allen shot out his hand and grabbed her shoulder. He pulled her towards him, as he had done when she had first threatened to ask the police to help. He seemed to have forgotten that Rollison was with them.

'You'll stay here and do what you're told! If you don't, you'll——'

He snatched one hand away and made as if to slap her across the face. Before his hand landed, Rollison jabbed a short-arm blow to the chin which made Allen's head jerk back. He staggered away from Barbara, who stood as if petrified, her face white, her lips parted. Rollison pulled Allen forward and repeated the blow, and Allen slumped down, unconscious.

Rollison stopped him from falling heavily, then slipped his hand into Allen's inside coat-pocket and drew out a foolscap envelope. Inside was a copy of the script which Rollison already had. There was also another typewritten sheet—and a glance told Rollison that it was the new version which Pauline wanted broadcast. He tucked the envelope into his own pocket.

'I think I had better get him away for a bit,' he said quietly. 'He's not himself, don't forget that.'

Barbara drew aside in tacit acquiescence. Rollison dragged Allen to the door. Sam was in the hall, and his eyes rounded.

'Knocked 'im cold?' he demanded eagerly.

'Help me downstairs with him, and then come up here— you're on guard in the hall for the rest of the day,' said Rollison briskly. 'Mrs. Allen will get you a comfortable chair. I'd rather you weren't here on your own,' Rollison added to Barbara, who nodded vaguely, uninterested now.

They got downstairs without being seen, and the cab was so close to the entrance that it was easy to lift Allen inside without the man in the street noticing. Rollison climbed in and Sam slammed the door. Perky started the engine and drove away at moderate speed.

Allen's head lolled back against the corner but he began to regain consciousness before they had reached Edgware Road. He blinked dazedly, sat upright and moistened his lips, then rubbed his jaw, which was already showing signs of swelling. He worked his mouth about slowly, but by then, there was an intelligent gleam in his eyes. Rollison would not have been surprised had he tried to get out of the cab when they slowed down at a traffic jam. Instead, he looked at Rollison with sullen hostility.

'Where are you taking me?'

'To some friends,' said Rollison. 'If you've any sense you'll stay there, and you'll be all right. Aren't you tired of being Aunt Sally for Blane and his mob to knock down?'

'He's not the only one who throws his weight about,' Allen growled. 'Barbara shouldn't—my wife shouldn't be left alone at the flat,' he said. 'It's too big a strain on her.'

'So you have flashes of sanity,' said Rollison.

Allen drew in his breath—and then suddenly turned his face away. He gritted his teeth, as if to prevent himself from breaking down, took out a plump silver cigarette-case and rooted in his pockets for matches. Rollison gave him a light.

'What good will it do if I go into hiding?' Allen demanded at last. 'They'll find me—they'll always find me. They're too strong for me and for you. It's best to get it over; let them have their way. Perhaps I'll be left in peace after that.'

'Isn't it time you told someone what's behind all this?' asked Rollison. 'And why Pauline wants you to alter your script for to-morrow night?' When Allen did not answer, he went on: 'This business appears to have started when you were half-way home from Burma. It followed something you did while you were in Burma. And it was something which made you more scared of the police than of Merino.'

'Who?' asked Allen, and added slowly: 'You said something about Merino before—who is he?'

'Blane's employer. Pauline Dexter's boy friend,' said Rollison. '*Haven't* you met him? He's the man who telephoned you so often.'

Allen shivered.

'No, I haven't met him, and I hope I never do. And—I'm not talking. It's my affair, I'm going to do what the girl wants me to on Saturday, and then I'm through. If they won't leave me alone then, I'll kill myself.' He shivered again. 'You may think I'm fooling, but I've never been more serious. I'm worth nothing to anyone. Bar looked at me just now as if she hated my guts—I know, I know, I asked for it, we needn't go into that.'

Rollison said: 'All right, you won't talk about what happened in Burma——'

119

'I didn't say anything happened there!'

'Then you won't talk about the reason for the trouble, if you prefer to put it that way,' said Rollison, 'and while you keep it to yourself, no one can do much to help you.'

'I don't want anyone's help!'

Rollison looked at him dispassionately, and could not feel much sympathy. Allen had become completely spineless—was sorry only for himself.

'I might let you have your own way if only you were concerned,' he said. 'But Snub——'

'Don't blame me for that! It's your own fault.'

'Anyone's fault but yours. Allen, I'm going on with this whatever you say or do. That's final.'

There was silence . . .

Allen stared out of the window.

'What are you going to do with me?' he muttered at last.

'You'll be told in due course,' said Rollison.

Allen didn't protest. He'd lost all self-respect and every claim to help, and—Pauline Dexter had helped to make him the wreck he was. Sweet Pauline!

Perky took the back streets and came upon the Mile End Road by way of the Minories, then, driving along another narrow street, eventually reached the rear entrance to the gymnasium. Allen, slumped down in the corner, showed no interest in where he was going.

Rollison opened the door and jumped down.

'I'll be back in a couple of jiffs,' he said, and added *sotto voce* to Perky: 'Keep an eye on him.' He wondered, as he entered the comparative darkness of the big gym, if Allen would try to take this opportunity to escape.

In the corner, beneath the only lights, the fair-skinned young boxer was going for a man who had the advantage of two stones, years of experience and two inches in reach. The youngster gave an astonishing performance, knocking the other man about the ring as if he were a sack. Bill Ebbutt, gripping the rope tightly, stared with glistening eyes without offering a word of advice.

Rollison reached his side.

'Cor, strewth!' exclaimed Bill in a whisper, as he glanced round, 'I told yer so, Mr. Ar, I told yer so—we got a champ there all right. Ain't 'e improved? Even in a coupla days, ain't 'e improved? Almost a miracle, the way 'e's improved.'

'He's certainly good,' said Rollison. 'Has he boxed in public yet?'

'Free times, before I got at 'im,' said Bill Ebbutt. 'Silly mugs, they'd 'a let 'im be knocked silly, all the guts would'a been knocked out've 'im, 'e wanted trainin'.' He raised his voice: 'Okay, okay, Willie, leave a bit of 'im fer 'is missus. I'll see yer in a minute,' he added as the boxers dropped their arms, 'go an' get a rub dahn. Not at all bad,' he added, for he was not a believer in excessive praise. Then he turned to Rollison. *'You're* givin' yerself quite a time, Mr. Ar, aincha?'

'One way and another, yes. Jolly phoned you about a hide-away, didn't he?'

'Ho, yes.' Bill grinned, displaying his uneven, discoloured teeth. 'I never would'a believed it, but Jolly's gettin' quite pally. Want the man ye've brought now to keep that dead chap comp'ny?'

'No, Bill, this one's alive. Young Allen. He might try to get away,' he warned, 'I can't quite make him out, but officially he's hiding away from the police and from a woman who's making merry-hell. If he does escape, don't stop him—have him followed.'

'O-*kay*,' breathed Bill.

'And I'll ring up for a report on how he's behaving,' said Rollison. 'Where are you going to send him?'

' 'E *could* stay 'ere,' said Bill, but shook his head when he saw the frown on Rollison's face. No? First spot the busies would look, I s'pose. Okay, then, 'e'll 'ave to go into Dinky's place. Know Dinky, don't you?'

'That'll do fine,' said Rollison. 'Same address?'

'Same address,' said Bill. 'Feed 'im up like a prince, I s'pose?'

'Just look after him,' said Rollison. 'I'll tell Perky to go straight there, shall I?'

'Better not use Perky's cab all the way, eyes at the back o' their 'eads, these flicking busies, an' you never know wot the flamin' narks might see. Goin' with him?'

'Perhaps I'd better,' said Rollison.

'Okay. Tell Perky ter drive as far as Old Wattle's,' said Bill, 'I've told Wattle to 'ave a van ready.'

Rollison nodded, patted Ebbutt on the shoulder, and went to the door. Before he reached it, Ebbutt was on his way to the dressing-rooms. Rollison smiled reflectively, then glanced into the cab and found Allen still hunched up in his corner.

'Old Wattle's,' he said to Perky.

'Oke,' said Perky.

The drive to 'Old Wattle's' took a quarter of an hour. They went through the dingier streets of the East End, passed row upon row of little houses, where children, some bare-footed and many of them in rags, played in the roadway and jeered and gestured at the passing taxi, and where women leaned against their doorways and talked with their neighbours and looked with furtive curiosity at it. Perky, who knew this district as well as he knew the West End, took a bewildering series of short cuts, drove under railway arches and down streets which looked as if they were dead-ends, skidded round corners, waved his hand at two policemen who were standing before a gaunt warehouse near the river, and eventually pulled up near a railway arch on which were the words: *'Wattle—Storage—Removals—Garage.'*

'Old Wattle' was a very old man who needed a shave and a wash, and who smoked a dirty-looking black pipe. He carried on a curiously one-sided conversation with Perky, speaking in a voice so low that Rollison seldom caught his words. As he waited, Rollison saw that all of the arches here were marked with the name *Wattle*. Presumably some of them were used as furniture warehouses; probably some were used, at times, to hide stolen goods.

Perky came away at last.

'Okay,' he said. 'Get in.'

He revved up the engine and drove into the railway arch, which was dark and gloomy, lit only by the day-light which filtered through from the street. At the far end were several small vans and pantechnicons. Two or three men stood about, one of them making tea over a gas-ring. Nearest the road at this end of the arch stood a small, plain van.

Perky jumped down and told Rollison and Allen to follow him. He opened the back of the van, Rollison and Allen climbed in, and the doors were closed on them. Allen gave a long-suffering sigh, but made neither protest nor comment. They sat down on a wooden seat.

The van bumped over cobblestones, then smoothly along good roads. The only light came from a circular window in the back. Rollison realised that the driver was taking a round-about route, to make sure that they were not followed.

At last they stopped.

'Here we are,' said Rollison.

The doors at the back were opened and a stranger—a little man in his shirt-sleeves—beckoned them. They were in a yard surrounded by high walls. At one end of the yard was a tall, Victorian house, an ugly pile which looked uninviting. This was Dinky's—an apartment house in Bethnal Green.

Allen stood blinking in the bright daylight.

'What do you expect me to do?' he growled.

'Just stay where you are,' said Rollison. 'I'll see that your wife's all right, and you'll be safe here.'

'You mean, I'm a prisoner?'

Rollison said: 'I mean you'll be a fool if you leave.'

The journey back to Wattle's took much less time than the outward journey.

Perky's cab was gone. Old Wattle stood in the shadows of the arch, pulling at his pipe. He took it from his lips and pointed the stem towards one end of the lane. Another taxi, older and more dilapidated than Perky's, stood by the kerb.

'Perky'll be seein' yer,' he announced.

'Thanks.' Rollison slipped five pound notes into a grimy, calloused hand, and Old Wattle acknowledged these with a nod. Rollison entered the other taxi, and Wattle watched it out of sight.

At last, Rollison took the foolscap envelope from his pocket.

He had already read the original script, which told a little of Allen's Burma ordeal. Brief though it was, something of his courage and endurance shone through. He read it again, thinking of Allen's behaviour now, wondering whether the experiences he had undergone were alone responsible. Allen had lived nearly four years with a jungle tribe, had suffered badly from malaria, had several times tried to get out of the wooded valley where he had crashed, only to find great mountain ranges hemming him in. The tribe had never been beyond the valley; it had looked as if Allen would never get out. On one sortie, he had broken his leg, and although all that he was to say over the air was that a native doctor had set it, Rollison found it easy to read between the lines. He remembered Allen's bad limp, due to that makeshift setting. It was a touching story of patient heroism during a period when Allen must have reached the utter depths of despair. In spite of his earlier disgust with him, Rollison felt his pulse quickening as he read the words which Allen was to speak:

123

'I'd lost count of time. I just gave up hoping. Then one day one of the natives came in, jabbering away and pointing at me. Others crowded round. I was told to pack the few oddments I still had by me, and get ready for a trek. Eight natives accompanied me. They made me understand that other white men were in the valley. I could hardly believe my luck.'

There the interviewer was to say:
'I can well understand it. And that was the end of your adventures?'

Allen's next words read:

'I wish I could say so. I don't really know what happened, but I assume my guides and I ran into a hostile tribe—and the other side had modern weapons. We were shot up. I escaped—the only one left alive. I thought that really was the end, but there was a party of white men—mostly Americans—who were making a documentary film, and I met up with them.'

'You just met up with them,' was the interviewer's dry comment.

'Yes. And they looked after me and eventually took me to Rangoon.'

'Well, I won't call you lucky,' the interviewer was to say, 'but we're all delighted that you came through, Mr. Allen.'

That was the final part of the original script—and the part which Pauline wanted altered. Before Rollison could study her version, the taxi stopped outside his flat. Rollison paid the man off and went upstairs. Was he right to blame Allen for his present frame of mind? Wasn't he much more to be pitied than blamed?

He opened the front door, and was at once astonished—and delighted—for Jolly was speaking to someone in tones of unrestrained excitement.

'. . . wonderful!' Jolly was saying. 'Wonderful! . . . No, he's not in at the moment but he will be shortly, and . . . Just a moment, here he is!' He took the receiver from his ear and beamed at Rollison. 'It's Snub!' he declared in high delight.

That was the first time Rollison had ever heard him call Snub anything but Mr. Higginbottom.

CHAPTER EIGHTEEN

CAT AND MOUSE

'WELL, Snub,' said Rollison. 'You all right?'

'I could do with a square meal and I've a bump about as big as a dodo's egg on the top of my cranium,' said Snub, 'but apart from that, I'm fit. My good luck! I don't know what's come over these people, Rolly, but they suddenly caved in.'

'Caved in?'

'Caught a wallop amidships and departed in pieces,' declared Snub. 'Bit of a anti-climax, but I can't say I'm sorry. They'd threatened all kinds of blood-curdling fancy tricks if I tried to get away, and I wasn't looking forward to another love scene with the girlie——'

'Which girlie?'

'Why, Pauline,' said Snub. 'She of the golden locks, the pink complexion and the black heart.' A subtle change came into Snub's voice. 'She's a very nasty piece of work. I've had the wind up from one breeze and another in my time, but she knows how to make it a tornado. And all so sweet and sugary, too. But you've been at her, haven't you?'

'I tried some new tactics,' said Rollison.

Snub chuckled, himself again.

'So I gathered. Until an hour ago she was all claws and blood-curdles, but she's become a different woman. Moral uplift from the Toff, I shouldn't wonder. She came to see me and didn't talk nicely about you, but I gathered that you'd done a bit of gun-spiking. You whisked Allen away from under her nose, didn't you?'

'More or less,' said Rollison.

'And does she want that lad to broadcast to-morrow! It's her one desire, give her that and she'll leave you the rest of the world. She emphasised what would happen to you and me if Allen were kept away from the studio—you wouldn't think a luscious lovely like Pauline could be obscene, would you? I was locked in a room in a small bungalow, near Guildford, heard a car move off, waited five minutes and then gave close attention to the lock. When I got out, the bungalow was empty. All she'd left behind her was her potent and powerful perfume. I always think you can tell the nature of the beast from the pomades, don't you?'

'Sometimes,' said Rollison. 'Where are you now?'

'In the bungalow. The exchange is Guildford, so——'

He broke off suddenly, and Rollison heard his exclamation —which might have been of surprise or alarm. Rollison's fingers tightened round the receiver and Jolly, his smile fading, stepped nearer to him.

While talking into the telephone, there had been a fatuous grin on Snub's face. It was partly due to the reaction from tension—for his experiences at this bungalow and at the garage in Lilley Mews had not been pleasant. And it was partly due to the fact that he was talking again to Rollison and letting himself go. He finished his story and heard Rollison say:

'Sometimes. Where are you now?'

'In the bungalow,' he said. 'The exchange is Guildford, so——'

And then he heard a sound behind him.

He swung round in the tiny, square hall, and saw the little man who was called 'Max'. And he also saw the gun in Max's hand. A small cupboard in the hall stood open; the little fellow had heard everything Snub had said. Snub kept hold on the receiver, but for a few seconds—precious seconds—he was petrified, and could not speak. Had he not been weak and weary from a sleepless night and lack of food, he might have done much better.

'Okay, I'll take it,' said Max. He held out his hand, and Snub backed against the wall, still gripping the telephone. If he threw it at the little man, he might knock the gun aside. He raised his arm.

'Now don't get violent,' said Pauline, from behind him.

She pushed him aside and took the receiver as it fell from his grasp. Max moved swiftly and hustled him away from the telephone, then stood back and kept him covered with the automatic. Pauline looked angelic then, and spoke in her most silvery voice.

'Are you still there, Rolly?'

'Good-morning again,' said Rollison heavily. 'Cat and mouse?'

'That's exactly what it is. You see, I'm determined that Bob shall broadcast to-morrow night, and I thought you might be persuaded to let him, if you had a word from Higginbottom.

126

We didn't go far, just far enough to let him think that he was quite safe from observation, and then we came back. He *does* look sorry for himself—even worse than you did, and you know how bad you felt.'

'I remember,' said Rollison.

'And of course you *might* trace the bungalow,' said Pauline, 'although I don't think you'll find it easy. I never think it's wise to stay in the same place too long, though, do you?'

'One gets into a rut,' said Rollison heavily.

'You're *so* understanding! We'r e leaving, as I say, and of course taking Higginbottom with us. At least you won't be able to say that you haven't had a last word with him. It will be the last word, if Bob Allen doesn't broadcast my version to-morrow. While we're on the line, is there anything else you would like to ask me?'

'I don't think so,' said Rollison. 'We're still even, my pet. I've got Bob and you've got Snub; we'll see whose bluff is the stronger.'

'I really don't care what happens to Snub,' said Pauline. 'Well, I must fly. I——'

She raised her hand to Max.

He took a step nearer the telephone, and let out an eerie cry, as if he were being tortured, and the cry broke off with a strangled gasp.

Pauline put the receiver back to her ear.

'*Poor* Snub,' she said. 'It's such a shame, and it's your fault really.'

Then she rang off.

Rollison did not enjoy the rest of that day.

There was no need to ask himself whether Pauline's nerve would hold out; it would. He did not seriously doubt that she would, if she thought it necessary, kill Snub.

Farran, Rollison's friend who had friends in the *Meritor Motion Picture Company,* called in the early evening. He was a tall, spare man with a beak of a nose and a bushy moustache. He had been able to discover little new about Pauline; she was being groomed for stardom and the general belief was that she would be a success. Nevertheless, she hadn't many girl friends, and that, according to the informative Farran, was not solely due to the jealousy which almost invariably existed between starlet and starlet; Pauline had shown an utter ruthlessness in the film world, trampling over any and everybody who got in her way.

'She looks as soft-hearted as they come, but she's a deceptive piece,' said Farran.

'Not your type, Rolly. I'm surprised at you.'

'I always like to try my improving influence,' Rollison said dryly. 'What about this fellow she goes about with?'

'Money,' said the friend, and sniffed.

'Not in the picture business?'

'Well, yes, in a way. Documentaries. Done some good stuff in India and the Far West, I believe. Just the man for *Meritor Films*.'

'Why?' asked Rollison, with quickening interest.

'Well, Meritor are documentary specialists. Done a few comedies but no feature films. Then Merino arrives with money— he used to be a jewel merchant—and Pauline gets a contract for the lead in *Meritor's* first feature. Curious fact, he took a flat above hers.'

'Very interesting,' said Rollison. 'Any little love-nest in the country?'

Farran raised his eyebrows.

'I wish I knew just why you're so interested, Rolly, she *isn't* your type. No, as far as I could find out, no one's ever heard of a country cottage. Town-lover and all that. She's been at the same flat for a long time, it was hers before Merino arrived. I can't get a whisper, apart from that. Sorry.'

'Thanks for trying,' Rollison said warmly.

'My dear chap. Pleasure! I say,' went on Farran, 'If you want a spot of strong-arm help I'm around and about all the time.' He paused, hopefully. 'No? Oh well, I suppose I ought to know better than to ask. Sure there's nothing else I can do?'

Rollison assured him that there was not, and Farran twirled his moustache and left.

'That is *very* interesting news, isn't it?' asked Jolly, who must have been very near the door.

'I almost think we're getting somewhere,' said Rollison softly. 'Allen was rescued by a film party sent out by the *Meritor Company*. Where are the studios—any idea?'

'As a matter of fact, sir, yes. They are near Epping Forest. But our first charge is the B.B.C.'

'Oh yes, but the more irons in the fire the better. We could ask——'

128

At that moment the front door bell rang, to herald Grice. He was spruce and brown and obviously prepared to be aggressive, for there was suppressed violence in his tone when he spoke to Jolly. He was astonished when Rollison sat him in a chair and proceeded to confess, without prompting, that he had persuaded Allen to 'hide' until to-morrow night. And:

'One or two of the other characters have taken a run-out powder, William! You don't happen to know how good the Epping police are, do you?'

'Very good, Why?' asked Grice, somewhat dazedly.

Rollison leaned forward in conspiratorial fashion, and tapped his knee.

'Could you tip them off to keep their eyes open for Pauline Dexter, who works at the *Meritor* Studio? One day she hopes to be an actress. Blonde, beautiful, brazen and bad boys' comforter, she may be somewhere near the studio with one or two extras or small-part players or technicians. I don't know anything much against the lady,' he added, 'but if she's seen around, and the Epping bobbies tell you, and you happen to let me know, I think it would show some results. On the other hand, if she or her entourage knew she was being watched they'd all run out on us. Savvy?'

'I savvy,' said Grice dryly. 'So, not satisfied with working independently, you now want us to help *you*.'

'Confound it,' complained Rollison, 'when I use Ebbutt's bruisers you complain; now when I come clean, you advise me to call on Ebbutt again!'

'I'll speak to the Epping people,' promised Grice.

'Now that's friendly,' said Rollison.

'But you can't go on like this indefinitely,' Grice warned.

He left soon afterwards, and Rollison sat back and surveyed the ceiling, feeling flat after the spurious excitement of the two interviews. At least he had now taken reasonable precautions against disaster for Snub.

He called Jolly, and took out the B.B.C. script with the copy of Pauline's alterations.

'Pull up a chair, Jolly,' he said. 'Let's see what we can make of Pauline's message to the programme's ten million listeners.'

'Or to a few among that number,' said Jolly prosily. 'Supposing I make a copy of the amendments, sir—we already have two copies of the original script—and then we can study them separately and compare notes and suggestions.'

'Copy on,' agreed Rollison.

Jolly was speedy on the typewriter, and instead of sitting back and studying the original, Rollison stood behind him and watched the letters leap on to the blank white paper. Thus he read more slowly, and the new sentences were impressed vividly on his mind. These 'new' passages were all at the end of the script, in those passages which Rollison had studied in the taxi.

Jolly typed:

ALLEN: I'd lost count of time, but kept hoping. I'd picked up a bit of the lingo by then, and one day gathered that a neighbouring, but hostile tribe, was coming to pay a visit. My little crowd was in a panic. They said this other tribe was armed with modern weapons, supplied by the Japs. My people decided to break camp. I slipped away from them during the night, and heard the fighting from way off.

INTERVIEWER: You were glad to be out of it, I bet.

ALLEN: Oh, yes. And by good luck, I found a way through one of the passes and met up with a small party of film people—mostly Americans—on their way to Rangoon after taking some shots for a travel film.

INTERVIEWER: You were glad to be out of it, I bet.

ALLEN: I certainly needed it. I shall never forget seeing white people again, after so long. I shall never forget their faces, either. I hope to meet them all again one day—the sooner the better. We've a lot of memories to share.

INTERVIEWER: You certainly have! Let's hope you find them.

Jolly finished typing, and took the paper from the machine. Then they compared the new version with the old.

'It looks very simple, Jolly, doesn't it?' Rollison said at last.

'In one way, sir,' agreed Jolly. 'It conveys a clear message—that Allen would like to get in touch with the men concerned, that he remembers them, and that *they* have something which they ought to share with him. Do you agree, sir?'

'I don't see what else it can mean. And if Pauline knows her job, she'll make sure that the people for whom the message is intended will hear it. They'll be warned in advance to listen to Allen that night, and they'll probably obey. There's a threat in the message too—that Allen would recognise all of them

130

again. I can't imagine the B.B.C. arguing against this, can you?'

'I see no reason why they should,' agreed Jolly. 'And I don't see how it would help us if they did.'

Rollison said: 'I think I do, Jolly.'

'Indeed, sir? How?' When Rollison did not answer, and by his silence exhorted Jolly to think, the latter went on slowly: 'We have only the vaguest notion where Snub has been. You know, sir, in spite of everything, I'm coming to the conclusion that we would be wise now to tell the whole story to Scotland Yard. *We* won't find Snub or the girl, but the police might. I really don't think you told Mr. Grice enough. Is there any other chance of getting results, sir?'

Rollison half-closed his eyes and looked at the ceiling.

'We can't find Snub, there isn't time and we haven't a clue. But we do know that Pauline is desperately anxious for this particular message to be broadcast to-morrow. She's gone to extreme lengths to make sure of it. Everything she's done proves that it's her priority Number One. And she told me that she would have a stooge in the B.B.C. studio who would make trouble if it weren't broadcast in this version. Right?'

Jolly did not speak.

'And I believe she will do that,' said Rollison. 'I think she's proved up to the hilt that she'll take any risk to get that message put over. And I think she'll send someone whom Allen knows to the studio, someone who will put the fear of death into him, to make sure that he doesn't get cold feet at the last minute.'

'Possible, sir,' conceded Jolly.

'Jolly, we must find Pauline or someone who can lead us to Pauline, or we're lost. If her stooge is in the studio, we must find a way to force his hand. But if we tell the police, they'll have to prevent the broadcast. Grice couldn't gamble on a quick showdown in the Aeolian Hall. If he did . . .'

He broke off at a sharp rat-tat on the front door which cut across his words. Jolly moved quickly, but Rollison reached the hall before him. He switched on the light and saw a white envelope lying on the mat. He strode to the door opened it; there was a distant scuffling movement; whoever had brought that note had gone. Rollison rushed downstairs and into the street, calling:

'Perky!'

He saw Perky Lowe's cab a few yards along, but Perky didn't make a move towards him. He thought he heard running footsteps but could see no one, for the lighting in Gresham Terrace was very poor.

'*Perky!*' He hurried to the cab, but still the driver did not move.

Rollison saw why a moment later. Perky had been struck on the back of the head, blood matted his hair, and he was slumped forward over the wheel.

Perky Lowe came round when Rollison reached the flat with him, and Jolly helped to carry him to the sofa. He vaguely remembered a man coming along the street and asking if he were free, but he wouldn't recognise him again. He'd said 'no' —and had then been struck on the back of the head by someone who had approached from behind.

'But never mind abaht *me*,' he insisted. 'I'm okay, Mr. Ar. You 'ad any luck?'

'I don't think so,' said Rollison, looking at Jolly, who had doubtless opened the letter.

'I'm afraid not, sir,' said Jolly. He took the letter from the desk and handed it to Rollison. Perky watched, with bloodshot eyes. Jolly stood erect and at attention, as he always did in moments of crisis. And Rollison read:

'The police will find Merino's body; and the gun, with H's finger-prints on it; and impeccable evidence that he shot Merino. But you can have the gun and the evidence after the broadcast on Saturday night, if it all goes well.'

'That settles the issue, sir,' said Jolly.

'We wait until to-morrow night, after the broadcast,' agreed Rollison.

CHAPTER NINETEEN

REHEARSALS

'OF course you can stay,' said Hedley, warmly. 'Very glad to have you with us, Mr. Rollison—thought any more about that broadcast of yours, yet?'

'Not very much,' said Rollison truthfully.

'I hope you will,' said Hedley. 'Quiet a minute, the tenor's going to sound off.'

He grinned and held up his hands for silence, and sat down on a slung-canvas chair, one of twenty or so which were ranged along the walls of the studio. The Italian tenor, a short man with a shock of dark hair, chest and shoulders like a bull, and plump hands which were clasped together nervously, spoke in frantic Italian to a much smaller man, obviously a foreigner, who kept pulling at his pink and blue tie and looking as if he would strangle himself. Another Italian, of aristocratic mien, sat at the grand piano in a corner of the large studio, his long, pale hands raised above the key-board. He glared at the pink and blue tie, and a compact, middle-aged man—a B.B.C. official with a patient, tired manner, kept saying:

'Now take your time, there's no hurry—this is only a rehearsal, remember.'

The Italians jabbered on; the rest of the people in the studio watched them or someone else, openly or furtively; or else read their scripts or stared with wide-eyed interest at the upright microphone in front of the tenor, the two table-mikes planted on small tables at one end of the room or—greatly daring—through the glass partition which separated the studio from the next room. Some were composed and poised, others obviously and unashamedly nervous. One little group of young people gathered in a corner and whispered.

Rollison sat next to Allen.

The tenor opened his mouth, threw back his head, and let forth a tremendous bellow. The patient-looking man jumped, the pianist clutched his head in horror, the blue and pink tie suddenly became unfastened, its wearer jabbered. Hedley jumped up and went towards them, saying mildly: 'That was a bit too loud.' The little group in the corner giggled, but the tenor seemed quite unaware of the minor consternation he had caused. He glared at the mike as if it would lean forward and strike him.

Allen stared at the scene with lack-lustre eyes.

Rollison had been to fetch him that afternoon, and as far as he could find out, Allen had made no effort to leave Dinky's; had eaten and slept and mooned about all day. For different reasons, Allen and his wife were behaving in exactly the same way.

Obviously he had expected Rollison to come for him.

Hedley had been busy with the tenor, and beyond greeting them with a bright smile and a few cheery words, paid them

133

no attention. The question of the alteration in the text had not yet been brought up.

Jolly was still at the flat, but was due to arrive here just after five o'clock. McMahon of the *Morning Cry* wasn't here yet, but Rollison had no doubt that he would come. He looked round at the others. There were nine in addition to the Italian contingent, and he glanced down at the comprehensive script, covering each broadcaster which Hedley had pushed into his hand, trying to place the people from their appearance.

The stage and screen 'comics' certainly weren't here yet; he would have recognised them. A young couple, with blonde hair and nervous smiles, were sitting on two chairs, touching hands, leaning forward every now and again and whispering; they were the young Danes, he hadn't much difficulty in placing them. A burly man in ragged and patched clothes, who had shaved badly and had long, curly side-whiskers, was standing in a corner, reading his script with a vast frown which wrinkled his forehead; he would be the busker, Rollison decided.

He glanced through the roneoed sheets. The 'wandering artist' or the writer of inn-signs didn't appear to be here yet—unless he was the pale, neatly dressed young man who sat by himself, smoking a new pipe. His name, according to the front page of the script, was Arthur Mellor. He was to broadcast first; the Danes were to follow; the Lundys were third, then came the busker followed by the tenor, with Allen the final act. Allen hadn't glanced at his script—just seemed prepared to sit back and do nothing.

The tenor suddenly burst forth again, still much too loudly. Hedley pulled the mike away from him, the blue and pink tie fluttered wildly and its wearer held his hands palms outwards a few inches from the singer, urging him backwards. The tenor tried to watch him, the mike, the pianist—and suddenly tossed his arms high in the air, stopped singing, and struck an attitude which he proceeded to justify with a string of fluent Italian—including, as Rollison knew well, one or two of the choicest Milanese oaths.

His friends pleaded with him. The tired-looking man raised his eyebrows resignedly, spoke to Hedley and went out into the mysterious chamber behind the studio. There, three or four men were sitting, one of them with earphones on and looking very earnest.

The altercation over, the tenor took up his stand again—

and suddenly everything went right. His volume was exactly what was required, no one disapproved, the ends of the blue and pink tie hung straight and its wearer achieved a seraphic smile. This was reflected on the face of the tenor; the pianist also beamed broadly.

A curious thing happened.

Everyone in the studio stopped whatever he was doing and looked at the Italian. In the small studio his voice was loud but the notes were perfect, and they flowed easily and smoothly, he swayed slightly to and fro, keeping his hands raised, as if without effort. The tenor's eyes were half-closed and dreamy, he were holding them out to some invisible maiden, appealing, beseeching.

Even Allen was affected.

Rollison fought against the seductive beauty of the singing and glanced at Allen, seeing his face relieved of strain—not smiling, but almost serene, as if he had been taken into a new world of peace. The tough-rough busker watched the tenor without blinking. The smartly-dressed man who was probably the wandering artist had his mouth open, and he also swayed from the waist. The two Danes held hands tightly. The little crowd which Rollison could not identify was the last to come under the spell, but its members fell eventually. Hedley looked dreamy. The weary-looking man, who wore a cream-coloured linen coat and flannel trousers, shed his tiredness. Two girl members of the staff stood near the piano.

The singer stopped but the spell remained, until he lunged forward and gripped one end of the blue-and-pink tie, and cried:

'*It was wonderful—yes, yes, wonderful!*'

Then he was submerged in a welter of congratulations from his friends. Hedley sent an inquiring glance towards the glass partition, where the earnest-looking man, smiling with quiet satisfaction, shook his head. Hedley turned to one of the girls and said *sotto voce*:

'We'll give him another try-out at the last minute, let him rest now.'

Another man came into the room, dressed in navy blue, wearing brown suede shoes, ruddy-faced, smiling and cheerful. Hedley called him 'Bill', and brought him immediately to Rollison and Allen. Rollison stood up, Allen hesitated before following his example. If Hedley and 'Bill' noticed that Allen seemed strained, they showed no sign.

'This is Bill Wentworth, who will interview you, Mr. Allen,' said Hedley. 'Mr. Allen—Mr. Rollison.'

Wentworth had a quick, firm handshake.

'Satisfied with your script?' Hedley asked Allen.

'Er—I'd like a few alterations,' said Allen. 'If—if that's all right with you.'

'Oh, of course,' said Hedley. 'That's easy enough, we'll have a look at it in a minute. Better give the young Danes a run through,' he added to Wentworth, and took him off, saying: 'Won't keep you a jiff. Now there's no need to worry,' he said to the Danes. 'Just read naturally, don't raise or lower your voice too much. The mike's "live" on both sides.'

'Live?' queried the girl, brushing her blonde hair back from her forehead.

'Er—it can pick up anything you say, even a whisper,' said Hedley. 'Speak into it, not to one side—keep a foot away. Don't let the script rustle too much, or the mike will pick that up, too.'

The Danish girl gripped the script tightly, until her knuckles showed white and the paper quivered violently. Her companion moistened his lips, stared at the mike and then at Wentworth, who had his copy of the script flat on the table in front of him. He was calm, friendly and reassuring. He leaned forward and whispered something, and then looked round.

'Quiet, everyone, please,' called Hedley.

A hush fell on the chattering Italians, but they continued to whisper earnestly near the piano. Wentworth opened with a summary of the organization which the Danes represented, finishing with the question:

'*And you like it here in England?*'

'*Oh, we do!*' exclaimed the girl.

'*It is wonderful!*' cried the boy.

Wentworth shook his head and sat back, tapping his script. Hedley raised his hands hopelessly and watched, half-way between the table and Rollison and Allen.

'I'm sure it's wonderful,' said Wentworth patiently, 'but you have to read from the script—from the paper. Now, look—I finish by saying: '*And you like it here in England?*' and then Hilda—not you, Hans, you come next, when I've spoken again. Hilda, you answer, just as it says on the paper. Forget about the microphone, just follow my words on the paper as you're told there—see your name?'

'But how foolish!' cried Hilda.

'I shall never do this,' muttered Hans. 'That thing—it frightens me.' He glared at the microphone.

'Oh, yes you will,' said Wentworth reassuringly. 'Now try again.' He read casually and fluently, and finished: '*And you like it here in England?*'

Hedley turned away from them, cutting them from Rollison's view, and bending low near Allen.

'We must whisper,' he said. 'Have you the alterations in the script?'

'Yes, they're down here,' said Allen.

'Let me have a look at them.' Hedley took the script and began to read, scratching his chin as he did so. Wentworth, the boy and the girl continued to read, and Rollison judged that they were still giving trouble, the girl dropped her voice too much at the end of every sentence, the boy had a tendency to shout.

'Still determined on doing the alterations?' he asked Allen.

Allen nodded without speaking.

'Anyone here you know?' asked Rollison.

Allen shook his head, then looked at Hedley, as if to say that he knew this man, whom he had seen when he had called on Wednesday afternoon. Hedley kept nodding, and began to read in a whisper. The Danish couple reached the end of their few minutes' trial and Wentworth raised his voice, while everyone in the studio relaxed.

'That was very good—very good indeed,' said Wentworth. He looked through the glass partition, and one of the people with the head-phones beckoned. Wentworth called to Hedley: 'Freddy wants a word with you, Mark—Mr. Allen ready yet?'

'No, we'll have to have the last bit of his script re-typed, it's been altered and affects your cues,' said Hedley. 'Peggy!' he called one of the girls and gave her hasty instructions, then hurried out of the studio.

'How are you feeling?' asked Rollison.

'Hellish!' growled Allen.

Rollison shrugged his shoulders, stood up, and walked across the studio to listen from further away to the burly busker who sat in front of the microphone with every appearance of confidence. From here, Rollison could also study Allen more closely. His forehead was still plastered and his face scratched, but his sullen expression was most worrying.

One of the girls came into the studio, looked about her and made a bee-line for Allen.

Wentworth, at the mike, began to read: *'Artists have the reputation of being unconventional people, and in the studio to-night is Mr. Arthur Mellor, whose pictures have been hung in the Royal Academy but who prefers to paint in a rather unusual fashion—in the leafy lanes and lovely villages of England. That is so, isn't it, Mr. Mellor?'*

The burly 'busker' said crisply:

'That's right. I dislike towns, and I don't see why pictures I paint should hang an the walls of houses where only a few people can see them. If they're worth looking at, then I think everyone, rich and poor, should have a chance to see them and if they're not worth looking at, they ought to be burned. I paint inn-signs—have done for years.'

Rollison grimaced to himself.

The burly 'busker' was the travelling artist and the neatly-dressed little man was presumably the real busker.

Then Rollison saw that the girl had given Allen a note; Allen was reading it, his hands clenched, his mouth tight. He gave an almost frightened, furtive glance, searching the faces of all the people near him, then looked back at the note. He crumpled it up and thrust it into his pocket.

The wandering artist talked on about his inn-signs . . .

Rollison let a few minutes pass and, when there was a break in the rehearsal, strolled across to Allen, who met him with a cold, hostile stare. It would be useless to ask him what the message said, and Rollison sat down as if he noticed nothing. They waited until the artist's rehearsal was over, and the well-dressed man approached the other table, where Wentworth awaited him.

'All ready?' asked Wentworth.

'Yes—fire away.'

'This is a world of queues,' began Wentworth, *'and weary queuers are often entertained by actors who prefer the road and the pavement to the stage itself. With us in the studio is . . .'*

Rollison slid his right hand to Allen's pocket, felt the crumpled paper, caught it between his middle finger and forefinger and gently drew it out. Allen was quite unaware of what he was doing. Rollison slipped the paper into his own pocket. The other girl came in, carrying some sheets of paper, and

Hedley took one from her and brought it to Allen.

'Just check this new script, will you?' he asked.

Allen read it and after a few minutes, Wentworth looked across at them inquiringly. Hedley gave the interviewer the sheet of the revised script, and Wentworth scanned it, then nodded.

'All set?' asked Hedley, and Allen went slowly, almost nervously, to the table. He sat down, and Hedley took the seat he had just vacated.

'Very nervous, isn't he—much more than I thought he'd be, when I saw him the other day,' he remarked. 'He looks as if he's had an accident.'

'He has, and it shook him up a bit,' said Rollison, 'but he'll be all right once the stage-fright's over.'

'Mike-fright,' corrected Hedley absently. 'Hallo, here are the Lundys.' He hurried across the studio as a couple in evening dress entered. The man was tall and good-looking, dressed in tails, a fitting foil to his wife, who wore a gown of blue sequins—a handsome woman. Neither of them looked like the comic turn they were on stage and screen.

Allen was talking freely enough, in a low-pitched, well modulated voice.

Rollison took out the note, and read: *'Don't forget you're being watched in the studio. If you get a word wrong, you won't leave the room alive.'*

Rollison asked the girl where the note had come from, and was told that a commissionaire had given it to her. The commissionaire had said that a boy had brought it in—and Rollison needed no more telling that the messenger had been Max. He went into the street, and saw Perky Lowe a little way along. He strolled to the cab. Perky's cap hid the adhesive plaster patch on the back of his head.

'Going places?' he asked.

'Not yet, Perky,' said Rollison. 'Are there any more like you?'

'Cabbies, yer mean?'

'Yes, who'll take a risk.'

'Make it worth their while?' asked Perky.

'Certainly.'

'How many do you want?'

'One will do,' said Rollison. 'Ask him to come here right away, and if Allen comes out, to take him on. You wait for four minutes and then follow if I haven't turned up. Is that clear?'

'Okay,' said Perky. 'I'll 'ave ter fix it wiv me mate, so's I can pick 'im up, if 'e 'as free or four minutes' start, but it'll be okay. Why Allen, Mr. Ar?'

'Just an idea,' said Rollison.

He returned to the studio, where the Lundys were at the microphone, cracking away and keeping everyone, except the Italians, in fits of laughter.

'Not a doubt they're good,' Hedley enthused, 'it's a good programme this week, isn't it?'

'Very,' agreed Rollison, and added as an after-thought: 'Who makes the Lundys' films?'

'He was just telling me,' said Hedley. 'They were with a Rank firm, but they're just going over to some new people, the *Meritor Company.*'

CHAPTER TWENTY

ALL PRESENT

THE studio clock on the wall above the glass partition showed that it was five minutes to six.

The studio itself seemed a different place. It was warmer, and there were more people; the friends and relatives of some of the broadcasters had come, and chairs were set a few yards away from the microphone, so that they could listen without walking about the studio during the broadcasts. Rollison detected a slightly harassed air in Hedley, Wentworth and the tired-looking man, as the hour for going on the air drew near, but they had succeeded in putting the 'performers' at their ease.

Everyone had been downstairs to the underground café and had tea; that interlude had helped them to get together. They now seemed like old friends. Rollison marvelled at the way in which he had come to know not only what the people looked like, but so much of their past lives. For each had rehearsed several times, until Rollison knew their life-stories almost off by heart. The busker and the artist were chatting freely in one corner, the Italians were congratulating themselves in another, and now and again the pianist strummed the keys. Hedley and the official staff were having a hurried consultation and looking at the tenor. The Danes, and several of the visitors, were chatting together. The Lundys and two other people in evening-dress were sitting in a row, swapping stories. Allen, who had rehearsed twice and seemed word and voice perfect, had lost something of his tension. Rollison, who had tucked the note back into his pocket, had watched every man and woman, every official who had entered the studio, but saw no one who appeared to take the slightest interest in Allen. Lundy certainly didn't.

Yet the note had been clear-cut:

'Don't forget you're being watched in the studio. If you get a word wrong, you won't leave the room alive.'

Little wonder that Allen was nervous!

He wasn't sure whether Allen knew who was here, working for Pauline, but every time the door opened Allen glanced towards it, drawing in his breath.

McMahon breezed in, caught Hedley's eye, grinned and nodded, saw Rollison and gave an almost imperceptible wink, and made straight for the Lundys. They obviously knew him. Someone asked what he was doing there and he turned the question aside easily.

Allen watched the newspaper man closely, suspiciously, having no idea who he was.

Rollison, now sitting next to him, asked quietly:

'Recognise anyone yet?'

'No.'

'Still determined to go on with it?'

'Of course I am. I can't hold out any longer at this pressure. Don't be a fool.'

Rollison said: 'All right. Let me have another look at your script, will you?'

Allen hesitated, then held it out, Rollison read it as Hedley came up to Allen with the tired-looking man who had a friendly twinkle in his eyes and who had not raised his voice or shown any sign of impatience during the early, trying period of the rehearsals. He was the producer.

'All ready for your piece, Mr. Allen?' he asked 'You've been word-perfect in rehearsals, and absolutely right with volume. You've a slight tendency to lower your voice at the end of a paragraph, and you might try to keep it up.'

'All right,' said Allen.

'I did wonder whether you'd care to start, instead of wind up,' said the producer.

'It would be over then—you're a bit nervous, aren't you?'

'I'd rather be the last performance,' said Allen with a sickly grin. 'I—er—I telephoned my wife and told her that I wasn't on until the end, she might miss part of it if I start too early. If you don't mind——'

'No, no, that's quite all right. It's just as you prefer.' The produced glanced at the clock. 'Ten minutes to go—Signor Toni, perhaps you will have one more rehearsal——'

'Si, si, signore.' Toni jumped towards the mike, gripped it, measured it, stared it in the eye and then took up his stance. The little comedy was played through again and went without a flaw, the purity of his voice held every one enthralled. McMahon looked at the Italian thoughtfully; in fact, everyone watched him, and so no one noticed the door open and Jolly put his head inside the room.

Rollison caught sight of him when he had been there for a couple of minutes, and immediately stood up and tip-toed across to him. Hedley turned and put his hand to his mouth for silence—Hedley and the producer were noticeably more touchy now that they were approaching the big moment.

Rollison whispered: 'What is it, Jolly?'

'I'm sorry to worry you now, sir, but I thought I ought to come,' said Jolly. 'Mr. Higginbottom just telephoned.'

'Oh,' said Rollison heavily.

'He said that we were not to be intimidated because he was in difficulties,' went on Jolly. 'But I gather from what he said, that he has been told to tell us to make sure the Mr. Allen broadcasts the new version. In fact, the woman came on the line and repeated her threat that we would not see Mr. Higginbottom again unless the broadcast went through perfectly. What *are* we to do, sir?'

Rollison said: 'We must find out who's watching Allen. There's no other way.'

'I suppose not, sir,' said Jolly. 'How—how do you propose to interfere with the broadcast, and make Mr. Allen say the wrong words?'

Jolly spoke carefully, as if he had difficulty in getting his words out. And between the lines, Rollison read his plea: 'Can't we let it go through? Can't we give Snub this chance?'

142

The producer came up and spoke sharply.

'Come in if you're coming, please—and no talking when the red light's showing, we'll be on the air then.'

'Sorry,' murmured Rollison. 'Far corner, Jolly,' They tip-toed across the studio.

Allen was on an end seat of the front row. He glanced at Jolly without any great show of interest, and kept looking hard at McMahon. There was much hustle and bustle in the studio. The artist was at one table, the young Danes already sitting at the other one. The interviewer would move from the first to the second table to carry out successive interviews, being given time to move by an announcer, who would speak for a few seconds between each 'act'. Only a few minutes remained. There was a sudden hush; everyone stared at the green light which glowed near the clock, waiting for it to turn red. A tall, good-looking young man arrived, one obviously known to the staff.

He moved to the upright microphone, buttoned his jacket, coughed and, without a glance at the script in his hand, began to speak.

He had been so casual that the others hardly noticed that the red light had replaced the green. In a voice so familiar that it seemed as if it came from a friend, he spoke briskly:

This is the B.B.C. Home Service.

Nothing happened when he stopped. Rollison looked about him in surprise, Jolly peered at the announcer, everyone waited and seemed to think some catastrophe had befallen the pro-gramme—and then Rollison saw that the announcer was look-ing through the glass partition and realised that the pro-gramme's signature tune, the *Knightsbridge March,* was being played on a gramophone in the control room. The tall young man turned away and began to speak again.

'Once again we stop the mighty roar of London's traffic and from the great crowds we bring you some of the interesting people who are In Town To-night!'

He stepped away from the microphone, and there was another silence while the *London Again Suite, Oxford Street,* was played over the air but did not sound in the studio. In the hush, it was impossible for Rollison and Jolly to whisper to each other. Then the wandering artist moved his script, coughed nervously, and Wentworth began to speak.

The programme was really on; in half an hour Allen would

finish, that red light would fade, the green replace it. Green for safety . . .

Jolly put his mouth close to Rollison's ear.

'You were going to tell me how you expect to influence what Allen has to say,' said Jolly. When Rollison simply looked at the back of Allen's head, Jolly went on: 'Are you *sure* it will be the right thing to do, sir? Is there *any* way of making sure that it will help the situation?'

Rollison said: 'Jolly, supposing we do what we're told—what will happen? Can these people afford to release Snub? He may have been on the spot when Merino was killed—we still don't know who murdered Merino, you know. It's even possible that Pauline will manage to fake evidence which can't be denied that Snub killed him. She's clever and cunning, and I wouldn't like to say that we can outwit her simply by giving way now and hoping to fight another day. Don't forget that she's put every-thing in getting that message put across to-night, and if she succeeds in that, then she's won. If we're to have a chance, the message mustn't go out, and we have to find who ever is working for her here.'

Hedley glanced at him, obviously disapproving. The Danes had finished, the busker was about to perform. In the control room several people were standing against the wall. No one appeared to be taking any notice of Allen, but the minutes were flying by, and his turn would soon come. Next were the Lundys, then Toni—seven or eight minutes at the most re-mained.

'Well?' asked Rollison.

'You're quite right, sir,' said Jolly, 'but if Allen is determined to do what the woman has told him, how can you prevent him?'

Rollison said: 'He's sitting there with his script rolled up, he won't open it again until he goes to the mike. Hemming-way's advised him not to read it too often. He'll be called to the table so that he's waiting there while Toni's giving voice. He might look through the script then and see it, but there's a good chance that he'll look on the first page and not turn over a leaf. Until he turns over, he won't see what I've done.'

'What *have* you done?' asked Jolly in an agonised whisper.

Rollison said: 'I've slipped back the original page of script —given him another copy. When he starts to read the second page, he'll be reading that original, and he'll be well on the way before he realises that it's not the revised version. He'll either

144

stop altogether, or pause and then go on reading what's in front of him. It's going to be a tense minute, Jolly.'

'Tense!' echoed Jolly.

Hedley positively glowered at them.

Rollison stood up, waited until Toni had started to sing, then tip-toed towards Allen. He ignored the frown of many who glanced at him. And Toni's singing reached a pitch of perfection which it was almost sacrilegious to interrupt. Rollison sat down on a chair by the wall, so that he could see everyone, including Allen.

Then he saw the door open.

He caught his breath. It didn't open wide at first, no one else noticed it, the Italian's voice drugged all of them—but Rollison watched the door, fascinated. Who would dare to come in now?

The door opened a little wider.

Rollison saw a hand gripping it—a small, gloved hand. Then a neatly shod foot and a well-turned ankle appeared; whoever it was, was dressed in black, with sheer silk stockings; he imagined Pauline's golden curls.

The newcomer stepped in.

It was Barbara Allen!

She looked swiftly round the studio . . .

Hedley had seen her, and raised his hand in urgent warning. Allen, sitting at the microphone, looked up and stiffened. Rollison saw his scowl— he looked then as if he *hated* his wife. No one else appeared to notice that anything was unusual, and the Italian's song came towards its end, a gentle, pleading end.

He finished . . .

'*And also in the studio,*' began Wentworth, smiling at Allen, '*is a man who has one of the most remarkable stories ever told, to tell us. He is Mr. Robert Allen, until lately Wing Commander Allen of the R.A.F., who was lost in Burma for several years—exactly how long, Mr. Allen?*'

Allen opened his mouth but didn't speak. It was only a momentary silence, no longer than that which had followed the introductions of the other broadcasters, but to Rollison it seemed an age. Now, too, he had to try to watch Allen and the others in the studio—and Barbara. She took in the situation at a glance, raised her hand to catch Rollison's eye and began to creep round the walls of the room. Hedley went swiftly towards her, to try to stop her, but she ignored him.

145

Hedley had no answer to such defiance, but looked thunderstruck. Barbara passed in front of Jolly, who leaned forward as if to touch her, then drew back. Rollison saw her moving out of the corner of his eye, but couldn't give her much attention, he had to watch the others. Some—the Danes, the young people who had come to watch, and the busker—were looking at Allen. The busker yawned widely; now that his part was over, he wasn't interested in anything, or anyone else. But McMahon, the wandering artist, Toni and his little troupe, the Lundys and their friends, were all glancing down at their scripts. Any one of them might be following the script line by line word by word to check Allen.

Rollison was trying to do that.

Barbara drew nearer.

He put out a hand, glanced at her and touched his lips, hoping that she wouldn't ignore him. He heard Allen answer another of Wentworth's questions, and saw him fumbling with the corner of his script, to turn over.

Barbara crouched down on one knee, beside Rollison.

'*He must do what she told him,*' she whispered in desperate entreaty. '*She'll kill——*'

Rollison gripped her wrist and held it tightly. Allen turned over the page. Two paragraphs were unaltered. The seconds which had passed so quickly before now seemed to drag; Allen appeared to weigh every word, as if he had difficulty in uttering it. His forehead was beaded with sweat, he kept rubbing his left hand against the seam of his trousers. Barbara was quiet now; she didn't move but knelt there without trying to free herself. Jolly standing up, looked towards the audience from behind. McMahon, also standing at the side of the studio opposite Rollison, watched everyone lynx-eyed.

Rollison wasn't looking at Allen now.

'*I'd lost count of time,*' said Allen. '*I just gave up hoping.*' He didn't falter, he hadn't realised that this was the original script. '*Then one day one of the natives——*'

He paused and looked up, sending a terrified glance towards the audience. Rollison saw that only one man, the actor Lundy, was looking at Allen *before* that pause, but a moment afterwards, everyone was staring at him. Hedley opened his mouth and gaped, Wentworth forced a smile, as if to say: 'It's all right, you're doing fine,' but the pause lengthened.

Lundy half-rose in his chair, and his hand was pushed against his coat pocket.

Then suddenly Allen began to speak, more quickly than before, but with every confidence, and Hedley relaxed, Wentworth wiped his forehead.

'. . . *came and talked to me. I'd picked up a bit of the lingo by then. Apparently a hostile neighbouring tribe was coming to pay a visit. My little crowd was in a panic. They said the other tribe was armed . . .'*

Allen went on firmly, with the new script, Pauline's script!

He wasn't reading; he was repeating something he had learned off by heart!

Lundy sat down again, few seemed to have noticed that he had moved. Wentworth said his little piece leading on to Allen's final paragraph, the message which Pauline had been so anxious that he should put over; and which was put over.

'*I certainly needed it. I shall never forget seeing white people again, after so long. I shall never forget their faces either. I hope I shall meet them all again one day, the sooner the better. We've a lot of memories to share.*'

He finished, and wiped his forehead. Rollison hardly heard Wentworth's final comment. Barbara was leaning against Rollison's knee, as if the strain were too great to bear. There was a tense hush—and then the green light came on, Hedley clapped his hands together, and said gaily:

'A minute to spare—couldn't be much better than that, could it? By jingo, it's been a good night!' He waved to Rollison. The producer came out of the control room and made a bee-line for Rollison. McMahon looked across at Rollison and shook his head reproachfully—obviously he thought that Rollison had deliberately fooled him. The Italians were shaking hands with everyone, the Lundys and their friends were laughing and talking. Allen sat where he was, as if he could not find the strength to get up. One of the girls took him a glass of water.

The producer reached Rollison, glanced down at Barbara and frowned, then gave a pleasant laugh, and said:

'I hope I wasn't too short with you just now; it's a trying time, you know—always the same just before we go on the air.'

'You were patience itself, said Rollison, 'I ought to be shot. Found it a bit of a strain myself,' he added, and then glanced down at Barbara. The producer took the hint and went to speak to someone else. Jolly hovered near. Rollison helped

Barbara to her feet. Her face was pasty-white and her eyes were filled with a horror which, a few minutes before, he wouldn't have been able to understand. But he did now, he knew the whole truth. Jolly could not restrain himself, and leaned forward so that only Rollison and Barbara heard what he said:

'So he knew it off by heart, sir. We've failed.'

Barbara said weakly: 'I must sit down.'

'No, we haven't failed,' said Rollison. 'I can see the whole story now, Jolly.'

'*What's* all this?' demanded McMahon, pushing forward and standing squarely in front of the little group. 'What can you see, Rolly? If you haven't a pretty good line in apologies, I'll never do you a good turn again.' When Rollison just looked at him, as if commanding silence, McMahon paused and frowned. Allen moved towards the door—he was walking with his head bowed. Hedley was by his side, commiserating, unable to understand why it should have affected him like this.

'You *know*——' began Jolly.

'Oh yes,' said Rollison. 'Don't let Allen leave, Jolly.'

'He must leave! You mustn't stop him!' cried Barbara, in a voice so loud that it sounded high above every other sound and made everyone swing round and stare. Even Allen turned from the door and looked at her. When she stopped the silence was profound.

Lundy broke away from his friends, and went to the door as if to leave hurriedly. He pushed Allen by the shoulder and opened the door with his free hand.

Rollison moved forward.

'Let him go!' cried Barbara, and flung her arms round Rollison and held him tightly, 'Let him go,' she sobbed. 'Let him go!'

CHAPTER TWENTY-ONE

WHAT HAPPENED IN BURMA

ALLEN went out, Lundy followed him, the door closed behind them. Barbara still clung to Rollison, but Jolly had hurried across the room only to be impeded by the Italian troupe. Hedley looked puzzled, but stood back discreetly. Rollison

148

put Barbara gently aside and went in Jolly's wake, but she wouldn't let him go alone, she clung to his arm and followed him. No one spoke to them, although someone called out: '*Shame!*' By then Jolly had opened the door and Rollison hurried out, dragging the girl with him. She kept saying the same thing over and over again:

'*Let him go, let him go, let him go.*'

Rollison said: 'Barbara, you've got to see this thing through. It'll be for the best in the long run.' He stepped along the hall, past a startled commissionaire. It was dull outside and a drizzle was falling. Jolly reached the kerb and Perky Lowe pulled up in front of him.

'As ordered?' he demanded.

'Yes,' said Rollison.

'Follow that cab, Lowe,' said Jolly, pointing to a cab which had just moved off, and then realised that the instructions were superfluous.

'Get in,' said Rollison. He helped Barbara into the taxi. Jolly followed and was about to close the door, when McMahon came running and swung into the cab as it moved off. A little further along New Bond Street the other cab was gathering speed. There was no sign of Lundy or Allen.

'Two of 'em got in,' said Perky cheerfully, shouting through the partition.

'All right, Perky—you just get a move on,' said Rollison. He sat back and took out cigarettes. 'It's all right Jolly,' he said 'that cab in front belongs to a friend of Perky's, I arranged for him to be at hand to pick up Allen.'

'I *see*, sir,' said Jolly; but obviously he didn't see at all.

'Now supposing you give me the stóry,' said McMahon.

'Shut up, Mac,' said Rollison. 'Think yourself lucky that I don't throw you out on your ear. Barbara, don't cry.' His words made Jolly and the reporter realise that she was leaning back with tears streaming down her face, making no attempt to stop herself. 'It isn't your fault,' he went on gently, 'you're not to blame.'

The words had no effect on her.

McMahon started to speak, then checked himself. He and Jolly sat on the tip-up seats, opposite the Toff and Barbara. Perky drove at a good speed towards Piccadilly, then to Trafalgar Square and along the Strand.

'Was it Mr. *Lundy*, sir?' asked Jolly.

'One of them is Lundy,' said Rollison quietly, 'but he was present chiefly for our benefit, Jolly, he isn't the real villain.' Rollison gave a harsh little laugh, and glanced at Barbara. She was still crying, stifling her sobs; and in the half-light she looked pathetic. 'Surely you know whom we're after, Jolly?'

'I—I'm afraid I do not sir,' said Jolly. 'It appears to me that unless Lundy is our man, then we have lost completely. Allen remembered those lines perfectly, he didn't have to read them.'

'He remembered them word for word although he didn't have a copy of the new script for more than a few minutes, he could hardly have read it, could he? Yet he knew it off by heart. I've wondered several times whether you were right when you first reminded me that nice, young women sometimes married bounders, Jolly. You were.'

'Bounders? *Allen?*' gasped Jolly.

'Allen,' said Rollison. 'I began to wonder when he went off with Pauline. He was at the flat about the time that Merino was murdered. And afterwards, he was adamant—he meant to broadcast at all costs. The way he behaved to Barbara wasn't just the result of overwrought nerves. His own fear of the police proved he had committed one serious crime. He was obviously prepared to do anything to save his own skin.'

'Allen!' breathed Jolly.

Barbara opened her eyes and looked at him through the screen of tears; and then she relapsed into subdued sobbing, she could not keep silent altogether. McMahon sat without speaking. The taxi bowled along the Mile End Road—and then turned off, heading for Bill Ebbutt's gymnasium; and Perky Lowe suddenly stepped on the accelerator and swung round the corner in the wake of the leading cab.

'Allen!' breathed Jolly again.

Rollison did not speak. The cab pulled up outside the dimly-lighted entrance to the gymnasium. Three or four of Bill's men stepped into the murky street, and the comparative quiet was broken by angry voice—Lundy's voice, which Rollison had learned to recognise while he had been in the studio. Lundy was protesting vigorously, but the driver of the first cab climbed out and suddenly it was surrounded by Ebbutt's 'boys'. Rollison opened the door of his cab and jumped down, saying: 'Look after Mrs. Allen, Jolly,' and Jolly was compelled to stay behind, whether he wanted to or not. McMahon jumped out nimbly and followed Rollison to the leading cab. By that time the protesting Lundy had been dragged out of the taxi, and another of Ebbutt's bruisers helped Allen out.

'Run through his pockets,' said Rollison, pointing to Lundy, and before the actor could protest, a man had patted him all over. This man drew out a pipe from Lundy's right-hand pocket; and Rollison knew then that Lundy had pretended that the pipe was a gun.

Rollison and Allen came face to face.

'What the devil do you think you're doing?' growled Allen. Clear out, and let me go home!'

'I don't think you'll be going home again,' Rollison said. He glanced at Ebbutt, who loomed out of the darkness. 'Get him inside, Bill.'

'I'm not going inside anywhere!' Allen rasped.

'Oh, yes, you are,' said Ebbutt. He stretched out a colossal hand and yanked Allen by the collar towards the entrance. Allen kicked out and tried to free himself but failed, and another of Bill's men came behind him. Allen started to kick and struggle, as if he were suddenly overcome by a frenzy. But he was overpowered, and there was nothing he could do to save himself from being taken into the gymnasium. The others followed in a little group—and Rollison, glancing out of the corner of his eye, saw that Jolly was escorting Barbara.

The big room was in semi-darkness.

Ebbutt and the other man released Allen, and he stood back against a punch-ball, biting his lips, glaring through the gloom at Lundy. And before any of the others could speak, he burst out:

'There's your man! Lundy! He threatened me while we were at the studio. He had a gun—I don't care what you took from his pocket, he had a gun!'

'Did he?' asked Rollison.

'It—it's a lie,' muttered Lundy. 'I—I had to pretend——'

'Pretend!' screeched Allen.

'You gave yourself away when you reeled off your new script so easily,' Rollison said. 'If you'd had any sense you'd have gone on with the original.'

'Don't be a fool!' cried Allen. 'I've often mugged up a piece in an hour or two!'

'But you only had minutes,' said Rollison, 'and that wasn't your first mistake, Allen. If you'd been loyal to Barbara in spite of everything else, if you hadn't played fast and loose with Pauline Dexter, you might have got away with it.'

'That's a foul lie!' snapped Allen. 'I've been a swine to Bar, but I couldn't help it. My nerves——'

'You *act* very well,' said Rollison coldly. 'You fooled a lot of people, Allen. Of course, you weren't putting on an act until you first went away with Pauline. She showed you a way out. Kill Merino, the man you feared, and share the proceeds with her. And you agreed. Since then you've acted very well—you were quite impressive at the studio. I suppose you took something to make you sweat realistically, just as you took morphia to make yourself sleep on Thursday and made it look as if you were still a helpless victim. And yet you probably killed Merino and——'

'I didn't kill Merino!' cried Allen. 'He didn't matter to her, she could have shaken him off——'

He broke off, and drew a shuddering breath.

Rollison gave a little laugh.

'Yes, time to stop—you know a great deal about the relationship between Merino and Pauline, don't you? But we're wasting time. Lundy, how did you come to be forced into this?'

Lundy licked his lips.

Allen glared at him, and burst out:

'You're trying to frame me—and so is Lundy!' screamed Allen. But you can't get away with it. It's crazy! I've been having a dreadful time, my nerves are all to pieces, but I've been attacked—look!' He banged his forehead with his hand. 'I didn't do that to myself, I didn't search my own flat. It's a frame-up!'

He stopped, gasping for breath.

Barbara stepped forward into the circle of light, and said in a montonous voice:

'I can tell you. He——'

'Keep your damned mouth shut!' Allen cried.

Rollison said slowly. 'This is one time when she isn't going to do what you tell her, Allen. She tried to save you even in the studio, she wanted you to get away because she knows you'll hang now that you're caught. But I think she's seen the only sensible thing is to tell all the truth. Barbara, when did you learn all about it?'

She said: 'Only—this afternoon.'

'How?'

She looked at Lundy. 'He—he brought a message, told me all of it, told me that if it all came out, Bob would be hanged.'

Once she began, the words came freely enough.

Ebbutt put a hard, restraining hand on Allen's shoulder, but Rollison was prepared for Allen to make a violent rush at Barbara as she spoke. 'And I stayed in the flat, trying to decide what to do,' she went on. 'Then—then I knew that I had to try to save Snub.'

Allen's hands were clenching and unclenching, his lips were working and his face was distorted.

'I learned—that Bob planned—to have Snub Higginbottom blamed for Merino's murder.' She turned to Rollison. 'Lundy told me that he was one of the party which found Bob in Burma. It was officially a film party, and Merino was with them. But they weren't just making films, they were looking for loot which the Japanese had taken from the Burmese and which was stored in a temple in one of the valleys among the mountains.' She caught her breath and turned towards her husband. 'And Bob had already found it. He was kept prisoner by the natives because he knew where these jewels were. When he broke his leg, it was in trying to get away with the jewels with a native who was prepared to help him.'

No one spoke when she paused.

At last she spoke again, in a voice so low that they could hardly hear the words:

'Bob knew that he couldn't do it himself. He sent the native with a message to a friend in Rangoon, a man named Maurice Fenton.'

Rollison remembered reading a letter signed 'Maurice Fenton', to do with one of Merino's big accounts.

'And——' Barbara began afresh.

'You don't know half of it!' cried Lundy. 'Merino and I went out with the rest of the group—you know some of them, Blane and Max, there were a dozen altogether. And we reached the village. There were hundreds of natives armed with swords and spears, a pretty tough job—but we tried to reason with them. Allen wouldn't stand for arguing. He'd got a machine-gun. The natives had found it, with some ammunition, and he'd rebuilt it, spent months doing it—and he mowed them down, he killed them in dozens!'

Lundy stopped; and no one moved or spoke, not even Allen

'It wasn't any good leaving some of them alive,' said Lundy in a muffled voice, 'so we finished them off, burned the huts down, and reported that we'd found the village set on fire by a hostile tribe—it often happens out there, no one was surprised. We got the jewels to Rangoon without any trouble, but getting them to England was a different matter. We divided them. Merino, Allen and I had the biggest lots, but everyone had plenty. They were smuggled back to England and the party split up, arranging to meet again when everything was safe, and the risk of danger was over. Allen fixed his story all right for the Press, same one as he broadcast. Then the trouble really started. Merino wanted the lot. He thought he could blackmail Allen into parting with his share, and get the others from those members of the party who still had some. He had a list of all the names and addresses—but Allen took it away from him.'

'*Allen* took it?' interpolated Rollison.

'Yes—so that he had the upper hand of Merino,' said Lundy. He talked eagerly, as if he were glad to get it off his mind. 'Merino knew that one or the other—Allen or Pauline—had taken it. There was only one, Merino wouldn't have copies made, he didn't want to be double-crossed. He plumped for Allen, that's what started the violence. And Allen had been scared stiff of Merino all the time. Merino had Allen kidnapped and beat him up himself, then sent him back for the list, but Allen had lost it.'

'That scrap of paper!' cried Barbara.

'Yes,' said Lundy. 'Merino sent Max and Stevie to the Allens' flat to look for that list. Only it wasn't there to find, because Mrs. Allen had destroyed it by accident.'

'Well, that's how it began,' Lundy went on wearily. 'Allen fighting Merino, and Pauline standing by, on Merino's side. And she saw that if they went on fighting, no one would get anything out of it. So she went to see Allen, and suggested they should murder Merino, collect all they could and get away from England. Allen fell for it. He—he'd come to hate his wife, he was just a savage brute by then. All he worried about was getting out of danger. He did kill Merino. I—I know, because I was there.'

A hush fell over them all.

'I couldn't break away, they had me where they wanted me,' Lundy said hoarsely.

'You mean you didn't break away,' Rollison said, and waved his hand impatiently when Lundy began to interrupt. 'It want to know one more thing. What was the real point in getting Allen into *In Town To-night*?

Lundy gave a mirthless laugh.

'That started as a joke. We used to listen to that programme when we were in Burma—listened to plenty, but that was the favourite—people in London while we were out there, get me? And I used to say that if we had to split up, I'd arrange to broadcast on the programme. They didn't believe I could fix it, and used to chip me about it every time the show was on. Well, when the list was lost, we had to get in touch with the others who'd got so many of the jewels. Merino first suggested the way. It had been arranged that Allen or Merino would dispose of the jewels, you see, they would all be prepared to part. But we had to get in touch with them. And I was pretty sure that most of them would listen to the programme. Fixing it was easy, I didn't even have to do that myself, Pauline did. Allen thought up his idea of fooling you with the altered script. After Merino was dead, you were the only danger. Once the broadcast was over, he thought there wouldn't be any more trouble. He and Pauline were O.K., he didn't see what you could do, because you would want to save your friend's life. He was going to get out of the country with Pauline, when he'd collected all the jewels. He wasn't going to share out the proceeds with anyone else. He had it fixed in his mind after Merino's death, that he only had to stall until Saturday, get the message over, and arrange a meeting with the others before he walked out on them. The truth is——'

He broke off.

'Yes, let's have the truth,' said Rollison.

'He's crazy!' cried Lundy. 'Living in a village drove him out of his mind. While he was there he just had one fixed idea, getting away with the jewels. When he got back, he wouldn't think far beyond it. I knew he'd bring us to this.'

Lundy's voice trailed off.

Rollison said slowly: 'I think you're right about Allen. His mind was turned.'

Lundy lit a cigarette with unsteady fingers, but the story had slackened the tension of the others. McMahon slipped away towards the telephone box, doubtless to reserve space in the *Sunday Cry*. Barbara looked dreary, and Ebbutt stretched

155

out for a chair and pushed it behind her. She sat down. Allen stood quite still, looking into Rollison's eyes.

'You're quite a boy, aren't you?' asked Rollison.

Allen said: 'Maybe I am. So is your precious Snub. And Lundy doesn't know where he is, doesn't know where Pauline is either. I saw to that, I wasn't taking any chances. What would you rather have? A rope for me and a bullet for Snub, or both of us alive and kicking?'

The only sound in the gymnasium was the heavy breathing of some of the men and, in the distance, McMahon's voice on the telephone. The tension had suddenly leapt to a high pitch again, and obviously Allen believed that he had a chance to win on this last desperate throw. His eyes met Rollison's in a challenge and defiance.

Then Ebbutt said wheezily:

'S'like *that*, is it? I bet 'e knows where Mr. 'Igginbottom is, though.' He took Allen's arm, and although Allen tried to pull himself free, Ebbutt gripped his arms and dragged him towards the dressing-rooms.

Five minutes were enough to make Allen talk.

Pauline and Max, with one other man and Snub, were in a cottage on the borders of Epping Forest, near the *Meritor Studios*. Rollison had telephoned Grice, who had been in constant touch with the local police; they made the arrests. It was over in a few minutes. Pauline was caught completely unawares—rejoicing in the success of the broadcast. She hardly said a word, not even to Rollison, who was with the police. She had felt so sure that the alliance with Allen would succeed, believed that Rollison had been afraid to go to the police.

Snub looked a wreck, but the merry gleam in his eyes showed in spite of bruised cheeks and a swollen nose.

McMahon was near the cottage when the prisoners were brought out—and later, when Rollison passed a lighted telephone kiosk, he saw the reporter inside.

Rollison opened one eye and saw Jolly with his morning tea and the newspapers which did not usually arrive so early on Sundays. Jolly said that he had been out, and handed Rollison a copy of the *Sunday Cry*. McMahon had been allotted a huge headline and a great part of the front page. Rollison sipped his tea and read . . .

Two hours later he went to the Marigold Club, which was not a haunt of vice, or a luxury establishment where the wealthy were mulcted, but a club for women. On its committee was Lady Gloria Hurst, the Toff's aunt. She had found Barbara a room at the club for the previous night. Tall and austere-looking, she received Rollison with a welcoming smile; for she was fond of him.

'How is she?' asked Rollison.

'As you can imagine,' said Lady Gloria. 'But she's young. she will be all right, although she'll go on making mistakes.'

'Mistakes?' echoed Rollison.

His aunt's eyes gleamed wickedly.

'She has a curiously high opinion of you,' she remarked.